Praise for

SON OF SVEA

"Lena Andersson's *Son of Svea* is an insightful dissection of the rise and fall of the Swedish welfare state, or 'people's home,' as it is known in Sweden. She writes with wry humor that walks the fine line between comic and tragic without ever putting a foot wrong. Andersson's keen eye for the subtle detail of many types of social mobility and the tragedy of different generations never truly connecting makes for a thought-provoking reading experience."

—Emmi Itäranta, author of *Memory of Water*

"Lena Andersson's precise, sharply drawn character types correspond to distinct groups in Swedish society, and her dry wit gently pokes fun at some of the downsides of the people's home, but with deep affection for it. *Son of Svea* does a terrific job of inviting the reader to see through the eyes of a representative mid-twentieth-century Swede, who would likely never be willing or perhaps even able to explain exactly how they see the world. It illustrates the Nordic concept of *Jantelagen* (the law of Jante) in a very engaging, wry way."

—Julie K. Allen, author of *Danish, But Not Lutheran*

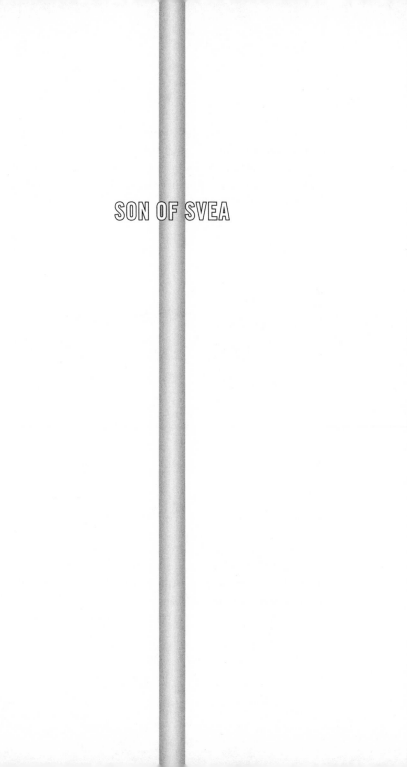

SON OF SVEA

ALSO BY LENA ANDERSSON

Willful Disregard
Acts of Infidelity

SON OF SVEA

A
TALE
OF THE
PEOPLE'S
HOME

Lena Andersson

Translated from the Swedish by Sarah Death

OTHER PRESS
NEW YORK

Originally published in 2018 as *Sveas son.*
En berättelse om folkhemmet
by Bokförlaget Polaris, Stockholm
Copyright © Lena Andersson 2018
Published by agreement with Hedlund Agency AB

Translation copyright © Sarah Death 2022

Translation of Evert Taube lyrics on p. 44 by Silvester Mazzarella.

Production editor: Yvonne E. Cárdenas
Text designer: Jennifer Daddio / Bookmark Design & Media Inc.
This book was set in Horley Old Style and Trade Gothic
by Alpha Design & Composition of Pittsfield, NH

3 5 7 9 10 8 6 4 2

Library of Congress Cataloging-in-Publication Data
Names: Andersson, Lena, 1970- author. | Death, Sarah, translator.
Title: Son of Svea : a tale of the People's Home / Lena Andersson ;
translated from the Swedish by Sarah Death.
Other titles: Sveas son. English
Description: New York : Other Press, [2022] | Originally published in 2018 as
Sveas son: en berättelse om folkhemmet by Bokförlaget Polaris, Stockholm.
Identifiers: LCCN 2021022303 (print) | LCCN 2021022304 (ebook) |
ISBN 9781635420043 (paperback) | ISBN 9781635420050 (ebook)
Subjects: LCGFT: Novels.
Classification: LCC PT9876.1.N35342 S8813 2022 (print) |
LCC PT9876.1.N35342 (ebook) | DDC 839.73/74—dc23
LC record available at https://lccn.loc.gov/2021022303
LC ebook record available at https://lccn.loc.gov/2021022304

ELSA

owards the end of the year 1999, an ethnologist from the University of Uppsala advertised for people—while there was still time, for their numbers were dwindling—to provide the raw material for her research on the Swedish mentality in the age of modernity.

At that point, Elsa Johansson was twenty-nine years old. She wrote a letter to the ethnologist to propose her father, a retired craftsman. His daughter was of the opinion that he was wasting away, leading far too quiet a life in Vällingby, in the northwest outskirts of Stockholm, where none of his considerable talents were being put to use.

Her father was so suitable for the research project, she wrote, that he would never dream of volunteering for it. "That sort of self-awareness would presumably disqualify anyone from what you are trying to explore. Your selection would be distorted if you only took people who think they fit your description."

Elsa was doing a PhD in linguistics and was thus rather preoccupied with problems of research methodology.

After three weeks, there was a reply from the ethnologist. She would be happy to meet Ragnar Johansson for an exploratory chat. It was only then that Elsa told her father about it. He was doubtful and disposed to be negative, but Elsa was prepared for this and had worked out how best to get him interested. She explained that it was to do with Sweden as a former role model for the world, about the nation's illustrious past, in which he had played a small but important part.

"If I can contribute something it might be a good thing, then," said her father, "though I don't understand what I could have to say that a scholar like that doesn't already know."

Elsa wrote to the ethnologist and suggested a meeting at the Pallas Café in Vällingby. The café had been there ever since they built Vällingby in 1954, when people came to visit from all over, to study a suburb of the future that had become a reality in their own age, thought-out in every functional, elegant detail as well as in the reverential effects of the whole on the democratic individual.

Elsa and Ragnar had found a seat in a dark corner by the time the ethnologist arrived, three minutes after the appointed hour, her eyes scanning the café. Elsa raised her hand to show where they were sitting.

"It could have been delays on the underground," said Ragnar, looking at his watch. "They get leaves on the line at this time of year."

The ethnologist was at the counter ordering, café au lait and some sort of bun that she seemed to pick at random after a quick glance at the cakes and pastries on offer. She looked harassed as she finally made her way over to the table with her tray, slopping coffee out of the cup and rendering her bun largely inedible.

Ragnar stood up, tall but slightly hunched as he held out his hand in greeting.

"Ragnar Johansson."

Elsa hoped the ethnologist was observant enough to register the essential little details, like the extremely distinct and confrontational way in which he said his name, like an assertion of something irrefutable that nonetheless required justification, and shook her hand. His hands were of the kind exclusive to those who work with them, with the thumb so far from the base of the index finger that the palm formed a perfect, rounded bowl.

She did not feel entirely certain that the ethnologist was seeing what she ought to see. The woman seemed underprepared, and was rummaging around in her shoulder bag for a notepad and pen.

Ragnar had a meringue-topped cake in front of him. This he returned to as soon as he resumed his seat, and with a concentration and zeal rarely seen in an adult put in front of a cake.

"I should have got here earlier," said the ethnologist with an unhappy look. "You weren't supposed to pay for yours."

For the second time she looked Ragnar Johansson in the eye, an eye in which there was not a single cloud of calculation to be discerned.

"So was it Stockholm University that was meant to pay?"

"The University of Uppsala."

"That would be from our taxes, then."

It was more of a meditative observation than a question.

"Why should the taxpayers pay for my cake today?"

He sounded genuinely baffled, as if faced with a problem he needed some help in solving.

The ethnologist appeared at a loss.

"Do you come here every day?" she asked.

"No."

Ragnar was now into the final third of his meringue, which he was eating as carefully as the previous sections.

"But I have coffee every day, of course."

He spoke slowly, his vocal pitch draining his words of interest. Sitting there, Elsa could see it would be impossible for the ethnologist to know that the slowness was the result of Ragnar Johansson constantly testing everything he said against some internal arbiter of authenticity, which checked that nothing false, illogical, or poorly considered crossed his lips.

As he consumed his cake in small mouthfuls, he kept his left hand cupped under the teaspoon while the right hand raised it to his mouth. Between each mouthful he took a gulp of his black filter coffee. There was nothing approximate in the way he ate his cake and drank his coffee, only a strange combination of systematic action and enjoyment.

The ethnologist had so far only taken one careless bite of her soggy bun.

"You went for a Karlsbader, then?" Elsa asked her.

The ethnologist looked down at her bun and turned it round as if expecting to find the name on it somewhere.

"Oh, did I? Maybe, I don't know. I just picked one that looked nice."

"Yes," Ragnar Johansson said to himself, "I like a Karlsbader. It's got that light crispness to it."

"A bit more like a Danish pastry than a bun," said Elsa. "Or a cross between a Danish pastry and an ordinary bun."

Ragnar gave a nod and added: "But there's a lot of fat in Danish pastries. That isn't good."

"Does it have to be classified so precisely?" asked the ethnologist, making a note.

"You have to know what you're eating," replied Ragnar.

"The ability to distinguish, demarcate, sort, and differentiate is the common denominator of all expertise," put in Elsa, with a mildly ironic and knowing little laugh, well aware that this was a matter of dispute in the academic circles of which she and the ethnologist were both part.

Then the ethnologist introduced her proposal and her subject. She was intending to write about the Swedish

"People's Home"* of the twentieth century as an arena for social mobility and processes of mentalization. It was just a pilot study for now, and there was no guarantee of funding.

Ragnar turned his guileless gaze out of the window onto Vällingby's main square.

"That seems complicated," he said, sounding as if he no longer had anything to do with life.

The academic explained that what she was looking for was still vague, although sharply focused in her mind. As a researcher, she wasn't allowed to be a metaphysicist, she said; solid empiricism was the only thing that mattered, but she still had to rely on her intuition for finding something she could make her empirical observations around, and she knew that what she was looking for did exist in some relevant sense of the word, and that it was important.

Ragnar looked at her and said politely but guardedly that he was sorry, but he couldn't help with difficult things like that.

"How many times a day do you have coffee?"

The question was cast out like a hook, not in the hope of any specific catch, but Ragnar was able to provide her with the precise information:

"Three times. At ten o'clock, two o'clock, and before I go to bed."

---

* *Folkhemmet*, literally "the people's home," is a Swedish term for what is otherwise designated as the Swedish welfare state.

"Every day?"

"With a bun," said Elsa, "always with a bun or something."

"Humph. Maybe a small cookie, nothing very much."

"Can you get to sleep if you have coffee just before bedtime?"

"I've never had any problem sleeping."

"He can't sleep without coffee," said Elsa. "Bitter filter coffee that's been left on the hot plate all day."

"There's nothing wrong with my coffee. The coffee's gone so damn peculiar these days. It sputters and hisses and gurgles and roars, and you can hardly hear what people are saying. It doesn't make it taste any better, either, and you don't get anything like enough in your cup."

Elsa remarked to the ethnologist that if she was going to write on this subject, she ought not to underestimate the impact that temperance had had on the coffee-drinking culture of the country people of Sweden.

"Where there's a horror of the effects of strong liquor on diligence and efficiency, relaxation and happiness have to come from other sources. So they introduced a comprehensive system of taking coffee with the famous 'seven sorts of cake,' and at very regular intervals."

"Do you think so?" asked the ethnologist dubiously.

She was clearly not remotely familiar with the description. Perhaps she came from a home with different habits, thought Elsa, where coffee and buns were not ritualized, where you drank red wine with your meal and rounded it off with an espresso and a chocolate with high cocoa content, the way Elsa herself now lived.

"Yes, definitely."

Ragnar Johansson was sitting there, lost in his own thoughts, one hand in his lap and the other on the table. It made him look slightly awkward.

It was Elsa who called Ragnar with the news that the research project the ethnologist had told them about was not going ahead after all.

By then he had virtually forgotten the meeting at Pallas, and was indifferent to this development. But when, out of politeness, he asked why that was, Elsa said it was quite hard to explain.

"There's a long answer and a short answer. The long one is that the ethnologist's supervisor criticized her from the word go for trying to reproduce essences in so-called reality outside discourse."

"That sounds complex. What does it mean?"

"The People's Home, for instance, which she wanted to write about as a kind of mental state, taking you as an example..."

"Yes?"

"It doesn't exist. The People's Home doesn't exist."

Ragnar cleared his throat several times.

"In what way doesn't it exist?"

"In the sense that it's a construct."

"Aha. Yes."

"She also said she had come to realize that Ragnar Johansson, i.e., you, didn't really have what was expected of contemporary research in her field."

"But I said that all along. I said it right from the beginning, didn't I?"

"Yes, you did. And that's why she's starting another thesis instead, on how, and I quote, 'the weakest citizens of the so-called People's Home were portrayed as aberrant and abnormal in parliamentary bills in the years 1932–45 and 1969–86.'"

"That'll be fine, I'm sure," said Ragnar.

"It'll get her a grant, at any rate. And a lot of attention."

"You know these things you talk about are way too difficult for me, Elsa. All these things you do. What was the short answer?"

Elsa gave this some thought.

"That you're too ordinary."

"Good," said Ragnar. "I'm happy with that."

RAGNAR

1

This is the story of a twentieth-century Swede. A man without cracks but with a great split running through him, and in this he entirely resembled the society he populated and shaped.

Ragnar Johansson was Swedish; he was the archetypal Swede. Elsa said that to him once, and he knew she didn't mean it as a compliment. Swedes found it ridiculous being Swedish, he had come to realize. The Swede was a country bumpkin of earthy simplicity. Those who voiced an opinion of the Swede did not consider themselves among his number but inhabited the thin stratum of abstractions in the air high above, where admittedly they spoke Ragnar's mother tongue but used it mainly for conveying to simpler souls precisely how simple they were, and how erroneously they thought and acted.

Ragnar's mother Svea's maiden name was the archetypally Swedish Svensson. Her brother's name was Sven. But ordinariness was a virtue, and Ragnar had no intention of apologizing for the fact that his mother's side of the family sounded as though they came from a primary-school reading book.

Sven and Svea Svensson were born, lived, and died in *Svea rike*, the kingdom of Sweden. As children they lived in Götaland, the most southerly of the three traditional lands of Sweden. In adulthood and old age they lived in the middle, in Svealand. Their parents' names were Johannes and Linnéa.

After their five years of elementary education in Glömminge, on the island of Öland, they were taken on by two separate farms in the area, he as a hand and she as a maid. When Svea was nineteen and Sven twenty-one, they traveled to the capital city together to look for work. Sven became a bricklayer, and Svea kept house for three rather well-to-do sisters in the smart district of Östermalm, where they shared an apartment on Narvavägen.

Svea was pleasant, dependable, and trustworthy, and within a few years she was married to Gunnar Johansson, the owner of a small haulage company. Sven, too, married above his station, to a woman from a farming family in the province of Ångermanland. Her name was Märit, and she had a lopsided mouth, which with nature's sense of proportion corresponded to a slight limp. There was also a hint of something corrosively surly in her manner that only corresponded to her deep sense of dissatisfaction, prompting suitors of her own social class to opt for other candidates. Märit Lind had to make do with Sven Svensson, an active trade unionist and member of the Swedish Social Democratic Party.

The girl from the solid farming background realized that with her congenitally crooked body she just had to make the best of it, but she found her husband's gracelessness and poor-man's ways such an affliction that she never let Sven forget that she had married beneath her, not him. The pair lived their whole lives in a tiny flat in the district of Abrahamsberg, with a kitchen so small that they could barely sit down together to eat. It was Sven who had to stand. As often as he could, he would go across town to see his sister Svea in Birkastan and eat her pork and potato dumplings, like they used to have on Öland. She would always make a vast number of dumplings, grating potato until she was worn out, and then they would eat them and talk about things only the two of them could remember.

Svea felt no sadness at exchanging Svensson for Johansson when she married Gunnar. The son they produced together, the subject of this story, was born the following year, year zero in Swedish history, the year Social Democracy came to power in the country and took over Protestantism's all-embracing mantle of care, severity, and the tendency for self-flagellation, both individually and collectively, which it would then occupy uninterrupted for forty-four years, fundamentally transforming Sweden.

Johansson's little haulage company did reasonably well, and Svea and Gunnar toiled from morning to night. On

Sundays they were able to take things a little easier, but the horses had to be fed and watered every day of the week, so they didn't get a proper rest then, either. Fear of the business failing was always there, but Gunnar was occasionally entrusted with some particularly responsible task, which lent a shimmer to their days—like the time he was in charge of clearing the snow in front of the main government building when the prime minister of Norway was visiting their own Per Albin Hansson. Gunnar was even in a photograph that was published in *Stockholms-Tidningen*.

Svea's husband was a contented man, satisfied with life and his allocated place in it. All he wanted was to run his modest business in a way that brought his family enough to get by. For a short period, they had two boys. The firstborn, whom they called Ture, was delicate and sickly and died when he was two years old, just after Ragnar arrived. Ragnar, by contrast, was strong and healthy, and already weighed five kilos when he was born.

On Sundays, Mother Svea was able to sleep in until seven and had plenty of time to sit over her morning coffee, thinking about things to the sound of the old wall clock, and then to dress in her best for the church service at eleven.

She had to go to church alone, because Gunnar was an atheist.

2

When the People's Home and Ragnar were both seven years old, war broke out in Europe. The same week he started in first grade at St. Matthew's School, named after the Evangelist. Mother Svea told her son that he was in a state of grace, being able to go to school, and should therefore never complain if it was difficult.

One day at primary school, Ragnar's teacher Miss Aronsson chose him to look after her lunchbox and the thin pancakes inside it while she left the classroom to see to something. Uncomfortable and full of foreboding, he put the lunchbox on one of the radiators beneath the tall windows. The radiator had a rounded top, and the lunchbox fell to the floor; the lid flew off and the pancakes landed among the dirt and dust. He stood there, petrified; his face felt hot and his body went all numb and prickly. As he scrabbled to pick up the pitiful remnants, he tried to think, and had the idea of dashing home to Mother Svea to ask her to make some fresh pancakes. But Miss Aronsson wouldn't be gone that long, of course.

He heard the other boys' coarse laughter. In their faces there was no sympathy, only pleasure in a break from the monotony, and relief that it was someone else's fault.

Miss Aronsson should have understood the blow that being chosen inflicts, thought Ragnar, and he would never stop thinking that. She had raised him above the crowd and told him he was worthy of guarding her pancakes.

It seemed unreasonable that you had to pay for your sense of order with shame and dread, but that was the way it was. Distinguishing yourself was too costly; you were entrusted with things that were too much for you. And he thought that as long as you were normal and blended in, you wouldn't make any mistakes.

The cause of your shame was what you had to divest yourself of. Being chosen. Being different. Being special.

At elementary school, Ragnar had a friend named Ingvar, whose father was an engineer. Ingvar was skinny and angular and knew from the start that he would go on to secondary school. He never came out to play football or ice hockey with the others, even though they asked him to, so they would have enough for two teams. As might be expected, Ingvar was already wearing spectacles at primary school, while Ragnar had excellent eyesight and well-developed muscles beneath his little layer of flesh.

On the ice on Lake Karlsberg, the boys had taken the initiative of clearing the snow from a rectangular area, where they played ice hockey after school while Ingvar sat indoors, reading. He was always indoors, reading. Ragnar realized secondary school wasn't for him. It was for the scrawny ones who caught endless colds and whose fathers were engineers. Because they were a different breed, the studying kind, who had no body and therefore no objection to never using it. Their body was just supporting material that hung down from their head and joined it to the ground so it wouldn't float away.

Mother Svea was sturdy and big-bosomed, and Gunnar was like a tree stump with an extra belly, while Ingvar's parents were small and so tinder-dry that you were afraid of them getting anywhere near a lit match.

It wasn't Ragnar but a precocious classmate who put it that way. Ragnar never came up with any bitingly witty remarks of his own, but he found them funny when he heard them.

"What would happen if everybody studied?" his father Gunnar used to say. "Who would do the work, then?"

Ragnar could hear that this was logical. He wanted to start at vocational college after Year 7, but Mother Svea forced him to study for an extra year. He had to stay at school for as long as he could, longer than his mother, who had so much wanted to keep going after the five years she was allowed.

———

Ragnar did not know anyone who attained greatness. Admittedly a few of the younger lads from Birkastan had made it as sports reporters for Swedish Radio, and he sometimes wondered what they had that he lacked, but he didn't know anybody in possession of true greatness. To dream of being great meant acknowledging that being ordinary was not enough, and he didn't want to do that. But in the winters he played ice hockey and was selected for two tours with the national junior team, and in football he set his sights on the top flight of the Swedish league. One summer he was loaned to the juniors of the big Stockholm club AIK by the local district team he played for. Everything looked promising. Lots of people thought he could go a long way in midfield, with his right foot, his stamina, his reading of the pitch, and his systematic approach to attacking play, albeit one with a predictability that made him easy for his opponents to read.

He thirsted for greatness in secret. He wanted to go a long way. But in a match at Stockholm Stadium he twisted his knee, down by the corner flag, and it was all over.

He didn't realize it was the end, so he carried on coming to training sessions for the rest of the season, on crutches, to support the team and show that he wasn't only thinking of himself. But when he had recovered and was playing again the following season, he was scared of breaking something. A scared player is no player, and he was dropped.

So as not to be the kind of person who didn't realize it was over even though others could see it and feel uncomfortable, he stopped abruptly, and sooner than he really needed to. He gave up without a fight.

And so it was that he left the clarity of sport for an existence in which people weighed one another on the scales of emotion and caprice. And there he would be found wanting. There he would fall short, he was convinced of it. There, too.

Both Mother Svea and her son lived their lives espoused to the view that people had to earn the right to live. But whom were they supposed to earn it from?

For Svea, this was a simple question. If you had received a gift, you were indebted to the giver. The main thing in life was to pay off that debt, not to grumble and grouse or demand anything for yourself.

Ragnar's reasoning was that if the gift-giver came in the shape of God the Father, it should be His task to tell the insignificant human race that they didn't need to earn the right to live. In a godless world, on the other hand, the main thing in life was not to grumble and grouse or demand anything for yourself.

It was a lie, he thought, that people had a right simply to exist, sitting there like a pasha to be waited on by others. The lie was formulated out of consideration for weakness, so it would never have to know what strength thought of it.

3

If he proved able enough, he hoped to become a cabinet-maker. He had shown unusual aptitude in paper modeling and woodwork classes, and now that the 1950s had dawned and Ragnar had reached eighteen, he was taken on as a journeyman by a master cabinetmaker, Erik Sköld. His qualifying piece was a mahogany cabinet in keeping with the contemporary fashion in furniture design, with severe lines and delicate inlaid work, its corners rounded to satisfy the eye's need for a little softening of all that severity.

His cabinet was superb, everyone could see that. It had drawers so well-made that you barely had to touch one side to close them. Drawers should glide, his master had told him; if they warped and stuck, they were incorrectly made. Ragnar's drawers ran with perfect ease.

He once happened to overhear the master speaking to a more slipshod apprentice and urging him to emulate Ragnar Johansson's discipline, even though he could never aspire to his feeling for form and material. The fact that this praise had not been intended for his ears made it all the more precious. For weeks, the master's words made his chest expand. The appreciation rekindled his hopes of greatness. But he soon started to think he had misheard, and worked all the more conscientiously so as not to let the praise blunt his efforts.

In May 1951, the cabinet was finished. With that, he had completed his vocational training, and achieved something of significance.

With the exultation rising inside him, he went out into that warm, early-summer evening and the almond scents of the bird cherry, walked by the water along Strandvägen, crossed the open spaces of Nybroplan, and turned into Hamngatan, up past Nordiska Kompaniet, the department store where he had recently helped renovate the teak escalators to earn some money while he was at vocational school. Then he walked all the way home to Birkastan, through the rough neighborhoods in the city center, with their shabby dwellings and their smells of misery and of a modern age that had failed to materialize, up Fleminggatan and past the Palace of Sport at one end of St. Erik's Bridge. Above the gleaming white Karlberg Palace over to the west, the clouds were pink and orange and looked as if they were playing a game of chase. It was one of those evenings when Stockholm was his, and the happiness pulsated inside him.

In October, Ragnar Johansson received his journeyman's license during a plush ceremony in the Blue Hall at the city hall. His mother and father were there, dressed in their best, proud and old-fashioned. He was embarrassed by their presence, though his thoughts dwelt not so much on them as on the building in which they stood. It was magnificent. Conceived and designed by a Swede of the world with whom Ragnar shared a first name.

When the ceremony was over and it was time to say their farewells, the master once more expressed his appreciation of his journeyman, adding: "It's a difficult line of work you've gone into, Ragnar, one of the most difficult."

And then he told him about a gifted apprentice he had once tutored who had not been able to cope with the competition, and had ended up in charge of the orders in a lumberyard.

"Many are called," said the master, "but few are chosen."

Ragnar's cheeks flushed red with embarrassment. It was as if the master could see inside him and sense his yearning.

The implications of the story tallied with what he had always known. In that instant, his decision was made.

Of course people of all eras would need furniture, but possibly not made of wood, which was on its way to being replaced by the new material, plastic, and he could not be sure that he would be among those making the furniture that people of all eras would need. There were no guarantees, and Ragnar wanted guarantees. He did not intend turning into one of those sorry individuals who fall victim to an inflated belief in their own abilities.

Another thing that people of all eras would need was knowledge, and this had the advantage of not being offered on the open market. Becoming a teacher was a bit like becoming a priest. God didn't change, and the church stood where it stood. It was the same with school, he thought; it remained impervious to the uncertain fluctuations of time.

Nobody nurtured dreams of becoming a teacher, Ragnar Johansson told himself, which meant the competition wasn't exactly cutthroat, and there was no possibility of failure. So he decided to supplement his carpentry qualification with the course needed for teaching: woodwork and metalwork for the democratic Swedish comprehensive school that had recently been brought in, and in which there was no tracking before the age of sixteen.

At the same time, he was invited to be the trainer of a football team in the Third Division, a distinguished old club that attracted a classier sort of player. Some of them were older than he was, and a number were studying at the Royal Institute of Technology or training to be doctors. This made him feel insecure and critical in a diffuse and defensive way. But as the trainer of a team he would be able to stay in close contact with sport, the only thing that really meant anything, so he accepted.

The trainer's role brought him some enjoyment, but the actual doing was the great thing, and he had abdicated from that. Instead of doing, he instructed. The teaching profession involved the same sort of abdication.

Ragnar was intensely aware that he was fleeing time after time to the dark corners where life was not lived to the fullest, and where he never had to push his own outer boundaries.

He opted henceforth to accept a life without aspiration.

The quiet tedium of a life in obscurity was most people's lot, so why should it not be his? But a chafing doubt remained. He wondered whether others were tormented, as he was, by the meaninglessness of not achieving anything, whether they brooded about obscurity and stagnation. And were constantly negotiating with them. It did not seem that way. His parents were not, but then it also seemed to him that he had more in him than they did, abilities that had given him good reason to entertain hopes of a wider sphere.

But the priority had to be on trying to make enough to get by.

He thought that political systems and ideas ought to take certain inevitabilities into consideration: people's options were narrow, in practice, and for most people, disappointment was built into the order of things. It therefore seemed to him irresponsible to encourage people to strive for things they could not achieve. Modern-day Swedish society had understood this better than others. Its whole basis was the unwavering curve of normal distribution, not notions of suspending the law of gravity.

A society had to induce each and every individual to fulfill their potential, but also to make them aware that this potential was probably not so great that they could realistically exceed it, and that it would only lead to unhappiness to try.

Ragnar's melancholy was shaped by his insight into the inexorability of the world. No hint of lightness danced within his soul; its color was dark, its key minor.

4

He found a job as a woodworking teacher at three schools in the new suburbs of Vällingby and Häs-selby, in northwestern Stockholm. The schools were small, and there was so little woodwork on the timetable that the post was shared between several schools. There he taught the children the basics of handling the materials, persuaded them to see their form as something fundamental to existence, encouraged them to smell the wood and feel with their fingertips how alive it was. He taught them to work *with* the grain and the life of the wood, not *against* them, tried to make them understand that a knothole was part of the wood and not a troublesome inconvenience, to see how the lathe could bring out the loveliest lines, and that none of this was gratuitous.

On Thursday evenings he would go home to see Mother Svea and his father and have pea soup and ham, but without Swedish punch, even though it was all part of the tradition. Svea was afraid of alcohol. She thanked her lucky stars to have found a husband who did not drink, which in turn meant he did not hit her. Ragnar was just past twenty-two when on one of his Thursday visits Mother Svea saw him open the refrigerator and take out a bottle of beer to have with his soup, rather than milk. There was always some low-alcohol beer in her refrigerator even though she knew it was the road to ruin, because unexpected guests might turn up, or clients of the haulage company, who had to be offered a ham sandwich and a beer.

"You'll find yourself craving it!" she cried, her voice full of anxiety.

Svea was aware of her son's irritation at her constant fussing over him, but still did not stop herself. The irritation was of a kind she did not understand. She had never felt that way when faced with anyone else.

"You'll find yourself craving it!" she muttered again, though she could see the strained look come into Ragnar's face. But her fear of alcohol was greater than her fear of his wrath. The haulage company had had an employee, a driver who always stank of alcohol and had no teeth in his head. Svea would pay him his wages, and two days later they would be gone. There was nothing left for his wife and family. They called him Olle the Soak. Svea's heart ached to see his wretched state but she could not help him.

And just a few weeks before the day Ragnar took a beer from the fridge, Olle the Soak had been paid his wages, and later that evening had fallen down the steps at Räntmästar-trappan on his way back from a drinking companion's up on Mosebacke.

He was found the next morning, his neck broken.

Ragnar drank his beer in silence. Alcohol was of no particular interest to him. It dulled the worry that accompanied his yearning to accomplish something of importance, but at the cost of distorting reality. Sugary foods were more pleasurable and produced the same feeling of happiness but did not warp reality, or involve any self-deception or lies.

In Mother Svea's home there was always a superabundance of sweet treats. Her showpiece was the checkerboard cookie. It was the most demanding item she baked, along with her shortbread meringue swirls. The simplest to make were farmer cookies, and they were always the last ones left uneaten, too. If they had guests from out of town, Gunnar always called them country cookies so as not to offend, third-generation Stockholmer that he was.

It was a long time since Svea had lived in poverty, but her memory of the hunger was like an all-consuming hole, deep in her marrow. For the rest of her life, she ate to try to plug it. Pure fat was what she liked best: cream, butter, and juicy bacon rind. When others cut the fatty edges off their meat in deference to the healthy-eating messages of the day, she would finish up what they left. Svea could never get enough fat.

It was because of her vivid recollections of poverty that her son, even when still quite young, carried a thin extra layer of subcutaneous fat, even though he burned off vast amounts of energy. Ragnar could see that the runner Gunder Hägg was as thin as a razor blade when he was in action, and that he himself was not, but he just thought that the two of them had different constitutions that meant they were cut out for different sporting disciplines.

In actual fact it was Svea's nutritious food that marked the difference between their bodies, and all those sweet things as well.

It would have been the most appalling defeat for Svea if her son had turned out skinny. Her cookie tins, pale yellow, light green, and old rose, slotted together in their three-tiered stack, felt empty to her if they contained no more than quick-bake cookies, rusks, and farmer cookies. The moment the tins were empty, she would get busy baking and restock them with shortbread meringue swirls, checkerboard cookies, raspberry thumbprint cookies, Danish pastries, cardamom buns, vanilla horns, crispy oat thins, and plain sponge cake.

5

f you were going into something that was not your dream job, the rational approach was neither to throw yourself into it body and soul, nor to slave away under an angry boss. The advantages of the teaching profession were the long holidays, being in state ownership, and the fact that you were your own boss in the classroom. Such were the rewards for the sacrifice of spending the rest of his working life at a level lower than the one rightfully intended for him.

So when the summer holidays came, he traveled. He went to Spain, because that was what people did and he was one of the people. It was a time when artists and writers were going to Paris in great numbers, but Ragnar was a craftsman, not an artist, and the Spanish way was more robust, less refined, more like him.

He loved the octopus and the sun, so unlike the Swedish sun, the white-plastered houses, the quiet of a village in the middle of the day in the quivering heat, the evenings with a warmth that made the air as thick as black velvet, darker even than the darkness of a Swedish winter. In Sweden, darkness and warmth never met, only light and warmth.

At home the darkness belonged to the cold, but in Spain it wasn't like that.

He went to bullfights in Madrid, Barcelona, and Pamplona, and marveled at the matador, keeping his urge to run away in check. He read Ernest Hemingway, because that was what people did and he was one of the people, and when he realized that Hemingway, too, had seen something in bullfighting, he felt an even stronger affinity with this writer with the pipe and knitted sweater who had liberated culture from its femininity by writing in direct and natural language that ordinary people like Ragnar Johansson from Birkastan could understand.

He actually wanted more meat and subject matter in the text than Hemingway's severe style allowed, but at least there were no strange words or peculiar references to people's spiritual lives. He was drawn above all to Hemingway's motto, *grace under pressure*. He intensely disliked his own outbursts of anger, which arrived so suddenly and raged through him like his body's own personal prairie fire. Rage obliterated his judgment and left him ravaged and devastated. He wanted to master self-restraint.

On his travels in Spain, he always wrote postcards home to his mother and father and the friends who were not on the trip. He was punctilious about that, Ragnar, and considered it important to keep it up.

At a bar in San Sebastián, his little party got talking to an American who was a college student and knew most things. He explained how to brew beer to give it the precise character of the beer in this bar, and he told the Swedes at great length what the distinguishing features of Swedish society were. Then he expounded on what bullfighting was really about: the arrogance of mankind.

Ragnar didn't like it. The American was too cocky, and it made him angry that even here in Spain he was hearing Mother Svea's lament on arrogance as the ruin of the human race, albeit in a swaggering American version. Moreover, it was wrong. Bullfighting was the very opposite of arrogant. A display of humility, a contest with no given outcome. It was the bull who weighed a thousand kilos, not the matador, and the bull was free to destroy his opponent.

He tried to say this, but his English was too poor and his Spanish was not up to the job, either, even though he had been attending evening classes all winter. The American peppered his speech freely with sentences in Spanish, though he was no more fluent in the language than Ragnar, and he then proceeded to inform them that Hemingway was overrated.

"Compared with what?" asked Ragnar, the English language lodged in his mouth like a block of stone.

The American faltered and looked uncomfortable. This often happened when Ragnar asked questions. Most people seemed to find it desirable for things to be shrouded in mist, he had noticed. If you approached a subject too directly, no one had any answers.

As he went to bed that night, Ragnar still did not know why Hemingway was considered overrated. He felt dejected for several days. Having finally decided reading was worthwhile, of course he had to go and choose an overrated writer.

"But he might be right about the bullfighting," said his traveling companion Benny, just as they were switching off the light for the night in their hotel room beside the river that snaked its way through the town. The little hotel was tucked away in a back street with a complicated name, which Ragnar had written down so he would not get lost.

"It is a very odd sport though, isn't it?" said Benny. "Going into combat with an animal so you can kill it."

Ragnar lay in the dark, listening to the surge of the sea.

"It's not about that," he said. "It's about the moment of truth. About not being able to run away. That's what bullfighting is. A human being is confronted with their own fear and there's nowhere to hide; all they can do is fight. The moment of truth."

He had bought posters of El Cordobés, the greatest bullfighter of them all. They were rolled up in his suitcase, and when he got home, he planned to put them up on the wall of his little bachelor flat on Västmannagatan.

"El Cordobés is the best at mastering his fear."

An attentive listener would have heard the particular stress he gave to the word *mastering* so as not to pretend the word was his.

"Does he kill the most bulls?"

"No. He takes the most risks."

To his relief, Benny did not ask any more questions, because he would not have been able to develop the thought any further.

"The moment of truth," said Ragnar into the darkness. "Not being able to run away."

Another evening found the friends from Birkastan eating calamari and drinking sangria at another bar, this time in Pamplona, in the company of some Spaniards they had met when they were running ahead of the bulls. The Swedes were sticky and flushed, and the lesser warmth of the evening was pleasant after the midday heat. Ragnar felt happy, and grateful for how wonderful everything could be sometimes, so he raised his glass and cried *"¡Viva España!"*

For him it was a jaunty exclamation, a Spanish idiom as foreign as any other. He was trying to show his appreciation for the land in which he was a guest, nothing more. But to his consternation, everyone around the table stiffened. Two of the party, a Galician and a Catalan, left the table in fury and went outside to soothe themselves with cigarettes and consensus, while Ragnar just sat there feeling crushed, and alarmed by the change in mood.

The young man from Madrid with the silky, well-tended mustache explained that Ragnar had just shouted out the watchword of the dictator Franco. It glorified Spanishness and symbolized the Central Powers' oppression of the periphery and intolerance of regional differences, local cultures, stubborn self-will.

Ragnar was ashamed and full of remorse, bright red in the face, even though it was concealed by the evening darkness. He apologized repeatedly.

But inwardly he wondered whether the Catalans and Galicians really saw themselves as so different from their neighbors that they could not obey the same laws. Or were the laws wrong for all Spaniards, in their opinion? What did they think? Were people the same or not? What was right in Madrid ought to be right in Barcelona, too, or else wrong everywhere.

The day a few years after the French Revolution, when Napoleon synchronized all the bells in Europe and they had left the madness of regional time behind them, was a great day, in Ragnar Johansson's view. He even admired Atatürk, the man who centralized his country in order to modernize it and introduce equality between the sexes and all citizens; who liberated women from having to hide behind the veil and who lifted whole groups of people out of medieval conditions.

So why go on about these regional differences in Spain?

He held his tongue as the questions mounted up.

He would long remember the uncomfortable atmosphere of that last evening in Pamplona. It had taught him a bitter lesson. You had to watch yourself and your surroundings, never drop your guard, if you wanted to keep censure and unpleasantness at bay.

A fter that evening, he started feeling foolish with his red scarf and white shirt and his fanciful talk of the blood and sand lending their colors to the Spanish flag, and about sitting in tavernas in the evenings drinking sangria and whiskey. It was an affectation, the whole thing; an attempt to turn himself into something he was not.

There was a reason why playacting was done in theaters, namely because it ought not to be indulged in anywhere else. Societies had to be built on the belief that what you encountered was identical to the way it appeared, otherwise they collapsed.

He was neither a Spaniard nor Hemingway, and maybe his whole excursion into reading Hemingway was phony, an experiment with becoming someone else. He was from the land of birches and cool summers, where honor and pride were not quite so important. He was the opposite of a Spaniard, however many posters of bullfighters and white stone houses in dazzling sunlight he bought to take home with him.

Under the scrutiny of his inner examining magistrate, he admitted that he had read Hemingway because one was supposed to, and because Ernest was strong and vigorous, although he was a writer. But in actual fact, he hadn't found the books all that interesting; he had never really got the point of them or grasped who was saying what.

He had secretly wanted to be an artist and had spent the evenings after work at home making jewelry, bowls, and ornaments out of wood or metal, which he then sold at market stalls or to shops selling arts and crafts. But before long the weather was too lovely for sitting indoors, and for the rest of the year it was too dark and dismal in the evenings. The enthusiasm he had initially felt faded away. It was hard commissioning yourself to make items no one had asked for, and besides, it seemed unlikely he had anything indispensable to offer the world.

In his soul he was not an artist, he knew that well enough. He lacked imagination and was too faithful to the laws of physics. What he produced was mere imitation.

All of this he acknowledged as his trial continued on the way home from what turned out to be his last trip to Spain.

From that time on he heard false notes everywhere and came down hard on them. Those teacher colleagues who did not admit that they had joined the profession for the long holidays, but claimed pedagogical ambitions, were dismissed with a snort of derision. He thought he knew that they were lying, to themselves and to others.

But, through the decades, the memory of Hemingway's titles stayed inside him like a Gulf Stream of warmth for adjacent, frozen land masses. *Death in the Afternoon, For Whom the Bell Tolls, The Sun Also Rises, A Farewell to Arms.*

He found them immensely beautiful. Had he enjoyed it after all, his reading of Hemingway, and genuinely liked it? Had the examining magistrate been too harsh in driving out every form of artificiality? Perhaps so.

6

When Ragnar dreamt thereafter, he restricted himself to things that could actually happen. He wished he could buy a summer cottage, so he set aside as much of his salary as he could afford each month, without giving up simple pleasures and daily cakes and cookies with his coffee.

By the age of twenty-six, he had saved enough, around seven thousand kronor, to buy a plot of land in Roslagen, close to the Sea of Åland. A sea view was too dear, but his plot was within walking distance of a bay leading out into open water, and that was good enough.

His plot of land was not far from places that Evert Taube had celebrated in song, and Ragnar loved Taube's songs. Every time anyone said the Swedish language was impoverished, and that was the sort of thing he heard often enough as a mechanical mantra from self-important, widely traveled people who knew that everything was better abroad and sounded more charming in foreign languages, Ragnar would put on a Taube record and say with a caustic edge to his voice: "Listen to this, and then tell me the Swedish language is impoverished!"

The lines closest to his heart were these:

How did you get this chance to go sailing,
with sun and fair weather prevailing?

Who gave you such a chance both to hear and to see,
to think, to write songs and keep singing?

And who decided you should be happy and free
like a bird on the waves ever winging?

So to mess up your job is not clever,
very soon you'll be sleeping forever.

Keep your ship sailing on, keep your heart beating
    strong,
while the waves are still sunlit, keep singing your song.

The words served as consolation every time he recalled his abdications, the fact that at the moment of truth, he had never stood his ground when the bull charged. His whole worldview rested in this song.

The plot he had bought was large and stony, and he intended putting a little house on it, along with a couple of outbuildings. His cramped and foul-smelling flat on Väst-mannagatan was abominable to him, and ought to be pulled down along with everything else now being demolished in

Klara. The old ways could not be saved, and it was nothing to grieve over.

From the abstractions of the higher stratosphere came the predictable message that hovels, drafts, and outside privies were charming. Their hatefulness to real people was of little concern to aesthetically sensitive souls of noble birth, as long as they were picturesque.

He loathed them, those scarcely fleshly beings who worshipped all things tumbledown, crooked, and dirty and who were now demonstrating, occupying, and marching to save saggy old rows of rot and decay. Their ethereal bodies and self-obsessed, bone-china souls provoked him to fury as he sat in front of the television set, seeing and hearing their dreamy pronouncements, slow yet still somehow shrill and reproachful, on subjects they knew nothing about. House building, for example.

Houses were not impressionist works of art; you built them with spirit levels and set squares. What mattered was for things to be neat and clean, firm and clear, and of service to modern men and women.

The house he intended to build for himself on the plot in his personal ownership would be just such a construction. No part of it would be put there at random. His house would reflect the fact that everything in the world hung together; sofa and beds would be built into the wall, and every detail would be conceived in relation to every other detail, meaning nothing could be changed without affecting the whole, as in an ideally planned society. No one would be able to patch and add to it in response to whims and new trends; the objects and phenomena would be locked together in a grip that was impossible to undo.

On his plot, Ragnar Johansson built a sauna in which the water scoop was made in precisely that kind of harmony with its hook, both made of the same wood that he had found in the forest nearby, and shaped to fit together so the scoop would never swing or clatter or be knocked off by mistake. It was hung at the right distance from the bench seat, so that sauna users merely had to stretch out a hand. Weighty at the base to lend stability, lighter at the top so it fitted comfortably into the hand. It was the definitive scoop, basing itself on divine forms.

Since human beings had the ability to perceive the existence and qualities of perfection—the ideal circle, square, or mazarin—and could easily distinguish such perfection from incomplete variants of the same objects, they ought also to know deep inside what the perfect society looked like.

It seemed to him as though the Sweden of the twentieth century was on course to be such a society. And his summer cabin would be something along those lines, too.

Everything in the cabin was made of pine, cut to measure and wall-mounted. He built the brick fireplace and chimney himself, too, although bricklaying was not his area of expertise. He sought advice on what he needed to keep in mind from his uncle Sven and an old school friend from St. Matthew's, who was now a bricklayer, and borrowed a book from the municipal library at Odenplan.

The librarian had to go down into a storage room to find it. Ragnar waited while she went to retrieve it and then found a seat in one of the reading rooms. There was a magnificent skylight in the ceiling above him. As he was reading, he looked up from time to time to see how it was made. The building was a combination of round and rectangular, light elements and darker ones. He had read in the paper that the style was known as neoclassicism and accorded due respect to the eternal forms for which Ragnar Johansson had such a weakness, even as he simultaneously worshipped all things modern. The modern age, to his way of thinking, was the epoch in which the human race attained the perfection that had been lying there waiting for it.

Having acquired some knowledge of the art of bricklaying, he set to work.

One sweep after another was later to express his surprise at finding such a solidly built chimney among the sixties' designs of the holiday cabins.

I f he had dared, he would have become an architect. Furniture was a sort of architecture on a smaller scale, with fewer risks. A piece of furniture could be thrown away or hidden when you grew tired of it. A house could stand for centuries and had no way of evading the passage of time or the critical looks of passersby. Furniture was private, the little life its preserve. Buildings were the public property of the eye. No mistake of any kind could be tolerated.

The architect was the highest of the high. Ragnar pronounced the word with a hard *k*, not a Swedish *sh*-sound, and took national pride in the world-famous Swedish architects Gunnar Asplund, Ferdinand Boberg, and Ragnar Östberg. They were craftsmen, engineers, and public ornamenters, all rolled into one. Architecture was the spearhead of modernity. It reached everyone, combining functionality with beauty, rationality with aesthetics, usefulness with sense of form, inorganic material with human biology. Buildings should be viewed with the eye but not solely that, lived in but not simply that.

It would have been too presumptuous to think he would be able to do anything like that. Ragnar was in many ways more frightened of succeeding than he was of failing. In every moment he wanted to recognize himself, which demanded a certain degree of restraint.

And now he found himself engaged to go round the schools in the northwestern suburbs, teaching children the simplest operations so they could learn to make butter knives, boxes, and enamel jewelry. He appreciated his more ambitious pupils, and one day a particularly gifted pupil, who was also polite and pleasant, came up to him in a lesson and said: "Sir, I'd like to make a secret compartment in my box."

This was not only a technically interesting problem; Ragnar also liked the boy's seriousness and his desire to do more than the task he had been set. But before he agreed to help the boy, he squatted down beside him so their faces were level with each other and explained that you should never hide things from other people and never do or make anything that you had to hide.

The boy looked worried, and replied that he needed a secret compartment to put his thoughts in, so his mother could not see them.

Ragnar stood up and said he would help him make a secret compartment that was so invisible no one would have any idea of its existence.

"What we want is a little spring," he said, and went to fetch one.

7

One Thursday evening, when Ragnar was round at Tomtebogatan as usual for his pea soup and pancakes, Gunnar declared that it was his and Mother Svea's most cherished hope that Ragnar would take over the haulage company when they were too old to run it anymore.

His father's words and the solemnity with which they were delivered filled Ragnar with distaste. Soon after that, the rage erupted. He gave them to understand that this was never going to happen, and told them what he thought of them for expecting such a thing of him. How could they presume to imagine it, when he had already selected his path? Didn't they realize that he wanted to choose his own life? Even if that meant a life of solitude, he had no intention of letting himself be burdened with their old-fashioned ways. How could they think he would want to take over something as tainted as a small, privately owned business; didn't they know him at all?

His parents did not understand, nor would they have understood even if he had tried to explain, that Ragnar Johanssen would far rather ally himself with the cool clarity of the state than with the family's cozy nook of smoldering injustices.

Dinner was a terrible test of endurance. Gunnar was a crushed and brooding presence, bright red in the face and breathing heavily. The pancakes Mother Svea set in front of Ragnar in frightened silence lay untouched, and the pea soup remained unfinished in his bowl. His father consumed the meal without noticing what he was eating, and without praising it as he did on every other day.

His disappointment at the response meant a greater distance between himself and Ragnar, a prolonged sadness that never entirely faded. But that was how it would have to be, thought Ragnar, even though it distressed him. He could not sacrifice himself for his father's sake; people just didn't do that any longer. Inherited firms like the haulage company belonged to the old world. In the future, struggling businesses like theirs would be sucked up by larger ones in a sweeping and effective move to rationalization. It was inevitable, and it was right.

The very week he had the showdown with his parents, Ragnar read a big report in *Dagens Nyheter* about the GDR, the German Democratic Republic. He noted that their flag replaced the symbol of the hammer and sickle with compasses and a sledgehammer—the symbols of the architect, engineer, and skilled workman, the tools with which the human race conquered the natural world and attained civilization.

The article referred to the wall that was being built to block off the West. In Sweden there was outrage, but Ragnar thought the arguments in favor of the wall had an irrefutable truth to them, and that was why everyone was getting so worked up: a country could not pay for its young people's education and everything else their lives entailed, particularly at the start, and then let them follow their own whims and desires, flap like sails without wind, and neglect their duties.

The construction of the wall across Berlin was understandable. If the state had paid for everything in your life, you were not free in your relationship to the state. You owed it something. That was how it had to be, he thought, and nothing else would be logical or reasonable. It was not acceptable to keep receiving and never give.

So ought he not to take over the haulage firm, in that case? He had been given everything by his parents, but now he wanted to follow his own path and let the business die with them. Did he need a wall around him, too?

He brooded and brooded. Then he talked to Benny, who was now a mechanic at a car-repair shop down on Torsgatan. Benny said that in a free country, each and every person could do what they liked, that was just the point.

"Yes, of course," said Ragnar. "But how do we justify that? Why is it right?"

"It just is. I wouldn't want to live in East Germany for all the butter in Småland. Would you?"

Unconcerned, Benny cast an expert eye into the depths of a Citroën 2CV that had just come in. It was the same model Ragnar had, but this one was green and his was yellow, and often in for repair.

"But there must be an answer to how we ought to think about this," said Ragnar.

To him, the question seemed unanswerable. Benny patted the car's bodywork and said: "Here's your answer. In this country, in France, and over in the States, you don't have to wait in a queue to buy a car. In the USSR they wait for ten or twenty years to get hold of a car. And then their choice is between one crappy little model that's barely drivable and another crappy little model that's barely drivable, both manufactured by VAZ."

"It's called a Trabant in East Germany, isn't it?"

"Yes. Like driving round in a picnic basket."

Ragnar was very fond of his little French car, and what Benny said sounded right. But he was still dubious.

"So why should the state provide its citizens with every possible thing of importance for free if they're then going to shove off with all they've been given?"

Benny wiped his hands on a dirty rag and they went into the little kitchen behind the repair shop for coffee.

"Look at it this way instead, Ragge," said Benny, adding three lumps of sugar to his cup. "What country has such low self-esteem that it thinks those who leave won't want to come back? Doesn't that show right away that there's something wrong?"

This, too, sounded like something Ragnar could agree with. But if it were that simple, the matter would be clear, and it wasn't. It was like a sort of itch in him, the urge to understand why people adopted varied stances on issues that ought to have definitive answers.

"But take poverty, then," said Ragnar. "Perhaps having to wait for a car for fifteen years is what it takes to banish poverty."

Benny started flicking through an evening paper, several days old, that had been left lying about.

"Or what about this," Ragnar continued his train of thought. "People who think they should be allowed to ride motorbikes without wearing crash helmets, just because everybody should be free to do what they want. Motorcyclists are often young people. If they have a fatal crash, they've cost the state loads of money but hardly had time to contribute any. So it can't be right that the individual gets to decide if they're going to wear a crash helmet or not. I mean to say, it can't always be someone else who has to pay."

"You're complicating this way too much, Ragge. It's what you always do."

Before Ragnar left, they agreed they'd go to the AIK–Degerfors match at Råsunda the following Sunday.

———

Ragnar went home and thought about it. When he had thought about it on his own for a long time, he arrived at an answer he felt to be unquestionable. The Soviet system was devised in such a way that it disadvantaged those with the means to leave, but advantaged those who had nowhere to go but had to stay.

There was a built-in psychological imbalance that cast socialism in an unfavorable light. When poor and ordinary people's lives were improved by rational use of resources, it was barely noticed, because they were not heard. They did not write books or newspaper articles, nor did they shout from the rooftops every feeling they had or every thought that struck them. But when the people of the abstract stratosphere, with access to the pens and microphones of whining complaint, when *they* found themselves slightly held back from their excesses, the world heard all about how painful it was to have to sleep on a pea.

That meant free countries had a built-in advantage in the battle for souls. Those doing well in such societies were the same people who were heard and could tell the rest how excellent their system was—for them.

So a political system that wanted to promote itself positively should ensure that the moaners, the writers, the speakers, and all the sensitive deviants were sheltered and coddled, whatever price the other citizens in society had to pay for it, because then there would be no audible complaints. As long as the loud, self-centered, and cantankerous brigade were kept happy, the system appeared good.

But how, then, could Ragnar sit back in the knowledge that his parents had given him so much and not meet them halfway? For his part, he demanded freedom. Was it because he thought parents ought not in fact be required to give their children all this and trap them in a state of perpetual debt, but that everything should be dealt with by the state?

He could find no way forward through the labyrinth. All his thoughts were blind alleys.

8

Ragnar's mother, Svea Svensson, grew up in the village of Rälla, on the western side of the island of Öland. The Svensson family lived in a single-room cottage where the drinking water froze in its pail in winter. When the howling wind swirled in viciously from the waters of Kalmarsund and tore off across the barren alvar, it made the uneven timbers and ill-fitting window frames of the cottage whistle and wail.

Svea was two and Sven four when their mother died of a weak heart, leaving Johannes alone with the two children. When he was at work, they were cared for by their maternal grandmother, Helena. She was nearing seventy, thin, tough and wiry, and born in the year elementary school education was introduced, but had had no schooling nonetheless. Johannes Svensson worked all day long in the fields belonging to the farmers of the fertile Mörbylånga valley, but could not make ends meet. In the end he abandoned hope of being able to stay. His income was too meager, the subjection too great, and many in the area had already left. He knew several of them, like Albert Jansson from Stora

Rör farm, Ruben Andersson from Glömminge, and Per Torkelsson from Rälla Tall.

The harvest had just been brought in, and it was harder to find work over the winter. Most of them had gone to California, to the fishing fleets and the stoneworks there, familiar territory for Ölanders. But Johannes planned to buy and work his own farm, and if it was true what they said, that Minnesota was like Småland, then that was where he would head for. He intended to take the ferry to Kalmar, then the train to Gothenburg and from there the Wilson Line postal steamer to Hull in England. Another train to Liverpool, which was where the boat to America left from.

The day Johannes Svensson set off, the trees were beginning to change from their summer colors and the honking geese were flying south over the Great Alvar in formations that had served them well for millions of years.

Svea went with him part of the way along the road to the ferry at Färjestaden. She was seven years old. Her father had asked her to open and close the first three gates for him. It was agony to part from the girl but they would soon see each other again, after all. Traveling with children was difficult and dangerous; it would be better for them to come and join him when he'd sorted things out over there.

Johannes Svensson was dressed in his best clothes and a shabby old slouch hat. He did not have much in his trunk. He was thirty-two and strong. Many had succumbed on the journey or after they arrived, but it never even occurred to him that he might not get through it. Svea was very anxious as his departure approached. The *Titanic* had sunk in April on its way to America, and it was a popular topic of local conversation.

When she opened the last gate, her father held the horse, looked down at her bare feet, gray with dirt, and then met her eyes, they, too, seeming filmed over.

"Farewell then, Svea," he said. "Farewell."

She closed the gate when her father had shrunk to a dot on the horizon. The landscape was flat, so it took a good while.

Svea never saw her father again, and no letters came, even though he had promised to write. Every day for two years they waited to hear from America, where Svea longed to go so badly that it made her breast ache. After a year had gone by, she realized her father had forgotten them, but carried on hoping for a year more.

While they were waiting to make the journey and join their father, Sven and Svea went on foot each day to the school in Glömminge, seven kilometers away, and when they got home in the evenings, they helped their grandmother with the chores. Svea very much liked the schoolteacher and everything he taught them. He never hit her, but Sven was spared neither the ruler nor the birch. Svea thought it was because he was so weak and timid; Sven seemed scared of everything. She had a more stable disposition, and was the one who led her sibling through every difficulty, although she was younger. When he cried because they had been orphaned and because he was hungry and because no letters came and because it was too cold in the house, Svea told him there was no point blubbing; if they could just get through it, they would be able to go to their father in America.

Grandmother warned Svea not to get too attached to the schoolteacher. He had dangerous ideas and spoke ill of the royal family, who had their summer residence not far from Rälla and would come riding past the cottage in a horse-drawn carriage every summer.

"You watch out for that awful social democrat," was her comment on the schoolteacher. "Watch out, Svea."

When news came through of the hunger riots up in Stockholm, Grandmother was afraid the king might be in danger. She had seen pictures in the local paper of Gustaf V standing in the courtyard of the summer palace to make a fine speech, and thought it a crying shame that the king of Sweden should be exposed to those bad people and their terrible behavior.

Johannes Svensson, by then living in Minnesota, had written just as diligently as he had promised, every month, and sent money for their passage. Grandmother Helena Pettersson had intercepted the letters and hidden them. She told the children Johannes was no doubt busy with his new life over there, and it should come as no surprise that his mind was on his own affairs.

It was not difficult for the old woman to justify her actions to the Lord, left alone as she was with two small children, and aware that she would soon be too decrepit to work. She did not want to go to America, and if the children went off and left her, she would end up in the poorhouse in Halltorp, twenty kilometers north, on the way to Borgholm. The prospect was very frightening to her.

At thirteen, Svea was taken on as a farm maid at Nytorp Farm; Sven had by then been a hand at the neighboring farm for two years. On Sundays they met Grandmother at morning service at Högsrum Church and then went home with her to Rälla for coffee and buns and handed over some of the money they had earned during the week.

Svea found the cache of letters from America thirty years later, when her grandmother Helena died, just after her hundredth birthday. The letters were in date order in three piles, tied up with sewing thread.

She read them in the order they had arrived. For four years their father had written to them, until partway through 1916, the year Svea turned eleven. His pleas for an answer grew increasingly desperate, until he finally gave up. "You are both still alive, I hope?" he wrote in his final letter. "I hope you are alive and thriving, dear children."

———

It was when Ragnar Johansson thought about Mother Svea's childhood that he began worshipping the state. He based this on its self-evident superiority to human beings. In the state there was no room for passion or apathy. When states did not function well, which was often the case in other countries, it was not because there was anything wrong with the concept of the state, but because of human failure in putting the idea into practice.

The fact that humans created by God were such badly functioning creatures in comparison to the just state created by humans seemed to Ragnar to be compelling proof that humanity was alone on the throne, without gods. Reason had created the state in its image. It was to human beings as thought was to instincts. Its principles of equality, clarity, and absence of emotion's caprices should be striven for, even in individual lives. Because each and every person merely feeling their way forward invariably found themselves in a place that they had never desired, despite having followed their own wishes at every step.

The state was humankind's better self. Solid. Exemplary.

9

Ragnar Johansson had two children in the space of three years. It was not intended that way, but then neither was anything else.

He met a woman at the Tennstopet restaurant, where he had gone on a night out with some friends. He was thirty-four and a bachelor. The general rule demanded otherwise.

The woman's name was Elisabet; she was just over thirty and seemed mentally well-balanced and independent in her ways. Beyond that, she possessed the positive quality of neither belittling her own statements with giggles nor greeting those of others with scornful laughter; she evidently took life extremely seriously. She came from northern Norrland and had not so much moved to the city as escaped to it, from the narrow outlook of village life.

This suited him well. He was as tired of the extroverted Stockholm girls as of his own craving for amusement. It led nowhere and was a false, slack side of him that he wanted to discipline and cut away. Admittedly when he was out enjoying himself, he was briefly liberated from his own austerity, but he felt shapeless. Now he wanted to reclaim the stability that sport had previously provided.

At that point, Elisabet was about to go to France to work as a nanny to a family in Lyon. She had organized it through an agency on Vanadisvägen, very close to her apartment in Röda Bergen.

She and Ragnar spent three nights together there after they met at Tennstopet. The third morning he called her Betty, and was sharply rebuked. She was not Betty to anyone. Elisabet was what her parents had christened her, and that was her name.

Elisabet Berg loathed pet names of any kind. Your name was your name, and you were who you were. You did not infantilize people by losing their names in babble. Not that she understood very much about social structures, or wanted to understand anything about them, as she would then have had to contemplate her own position in the hierarchy, but it nonetheless seemed to her that high and low were united in an undermining of human dignity by the deplorable habit of using diminutives that turned adults into children and people into pets.

She made it clear to Ragnar Johansson that she would never ever call him Ragge, as she had heard his friends do. He took this as a declaration of love and an announcement of their engagement, as there seemed to be a prospect that their association would continue for a period of time so long that the word *ever* was appropriate.

He was not very keen on pet names himself, but in order not to appear too particular or odd he had allowed distortions of his name. He could stop that now, bolstered by the firmness of her principles. The second time they met, he asked if she spelled her name with an *h*, to which she declared with the same emphatic indignation as she had in the face of the diminutive that there were no grounds whatsoever for having superfluous letters in your name. With a gentle laugh, Ragnar said that people did in fact act irrationally sometimes.

Those who adopted new names were another abomination in Elisabet Berg's eyes. In the 1950s, every other person changed their commonplace but honest surname to something artificial and more individual. It nearly always ended up sounding hideous, and so obviously an adopted name that it was akin to the embarrassment of wearing a wig—a bad wig, at that. Each time Elisabet saw an unnatural name, her voice took on a more acid tone.

"There goes someone," she would say, "who used to be called Andersson or Persson or Johansson."

She made it sound as though she had ripped the mask from the upstart and the borrowed feathers from the climber. Unjustified pretensions were the worst thing Elisabet Berg knew. She and Ragnar got on very well.

So, two months after they met, Elisabet went off to Lyon for a further six. That is no time at all to wait in normal circumstances, or for someone with a wrong to avenge, but for a person in love it is longer than eternity. Ragnar secretly wished she would call off the trip, or annul it, as she would have said. Elisabet took great pride in her rich vocabulary and enjoyed exploiting it.

But she took no steps to annul it and did not seem to have considered such action. Nor did he detect any anguish in her at the prospect of leaving, or the slightest concern about losing him. This bewildered him, but he put a brave face on it. He had never nurtured hopes of anything magnificent where love was concerned; you had to be content with the way things went and what proved possible.

Had the situation been the reverse, he would have canceled the trip, he felt sure, but the situation could not have been the reverse, for he felt no urge to go abroad. The holidays to Spain had filled his quota for good.

Elisabet Berg was like no woman he had met before. Chatty yet hard as flint, an unusual combination, and ashamed of feelings and desires and all the other needs that made her dependent. But the moments when the chatter turned to reflection and the flint softened were of great value, so he intended to wait for her.

Elisabet, for her part, must surely have found time to be attracted to Ragnar and his forceful presence in the rooms he entered, although not as attracted as she was to her single-minded plans to see the world. She felt a need to learn languages and make herself cosmopolitan as part of digging up, destroying, and erasing her rural roots. She had been working for many years, toiling away at regular jobs and extra jobs to save enough money for her trips, determined not to let herself be distracted. She had no intention of giving up work even if she got married; she had known this since she was a child.

At the same time, she had an old-fashioned approach to morality and convention. This Ragnar had noted with tender surprise as she lay in his arms and talked about the world and herself in it, her parents up in Norrbotten, her siblings, who had all stayed there, too. She told him she did not like the condescending and dismissive way in which he referred to his parents, like dead meat from a bygone age.

She was a product of the nineteenth century crossed with a woman of the sixties, with short hair, black-and-white checkered trousers, and a matching cap.

Her moral compass had been set in the century and the part of the country that had nurtured her much-loved parents, a part of the country that went with her like a birthmark, for others to inspect and for her to conceal. She tried to get rid of her accent, but it came through in every syllable. It exasperated her that Swedes from the south took liberties she did not feel were open to her. The Smålanders, Dalarna-dwellers, Scanians, and Hallanders did not seem to feel the need to make an effort to wash away their dialects.

She would feel offended and dejected whenever anyone asked her where she came from, or expressed warm appreciation of the famed clear diction of the Norrlander, while remarking that you could really tell she came from up north.

To come from up north was the very worst, she imagined everyone must think, the most boorish of all Swedish varieties of boorishness. Elisabet Berg took it for granted that there was unanimity on that point.

Her teachers at secondary school had all come from down south, speaking Standard Swedish with no dialect, possibly with a faint accent from some southerly part of the country but nothing that could tie those teachers in the back of beyond to any specific place. They were the servants and nationwide teachers of the new democratic state. Wherever in the land their knowledge was required, there they would go, taking their everlasting erudition with them and carrying out their mission.

Once, a teacher came up to Elisabet after break time. It was Mr. Strömberg, who taught her Swedish and history. He had given her some reading recommendations, books that she then borrowed from the public library and read with a flashlight under the bedclothes so no one at home would notice. Elisabet very much liked Mr. Strömberg, who knew everything about literature from Homer onward, and drilled his students in grammar. To have had him for Swedish and not be able to describe the function of the direct object in a sentence or the characteristics of an adverbial of time was simply impossible.

Mr. Strömberg put his hand on Elisabet's shoulder and said: "Elisabet, I heard you just now during break. I didn't know you spoke like that outside the classroom. You must stop that. You're to speak Swedish, not double Dutch. You're a clever girl, so you understand why. If you're going to get anywhere, you have to speak Standard Swedish."

Elisabet felt embarrassed. Mr. Strömberg's exhortation was earnestly meant and for her own good. Educated people, she realized, saw simple minds and a language without refinement in her northerly province. Let everyone who left that place expunge all trace of it, she thought. So they did not disgrace one another. Disgrace her.

In the six months Elisabet was in Lyon, they wrote each other letters. He wrote that the city he loved no longer looked the way it used to before he met her; the buildings had lost their luster and the streets were drearily gray. Not even city hall was quite itself.

She wrote that Lyon was a fabulously interesting city.

He wrote that every Thursday he went to see Mother Svea and his father for pea soup, ham, and pancakes as usual, and on Sundays he went to continue building his house, which he hoped to show her one day. He looked forward to that day so fervently that his bones creaked and his groin tingled, but he did not write about that.

She wrote that she had eaten the most exquisite coq au vin at one of the city's restaurants, and that she looked forward to helping him with the stone wall round the summerhouse plot.

Elisabet Berg did not curtail her visit by a single day. But the second person she telephoned on her return was Ragnar. The first call went to her mother, back home in the village.

It was raining steadily in Stockholm that weekend, but he did not take an umbrella with him as he rushed off to her one-room flat with its cupboard kitchen. All his clothes were left to dry on the radiator for the remainder of the day.

10

Elisabet Berg thought she had been very careful about the Pill. For a few anguished days she saw her life closing round the confines of a woman's small tasks. She quietly contemplated a trip to Poland, but any form of intervention in her lower abdomen, and, moreover, any intervention done behind the Iron Curtain at the hands of a Pole, seemed even more terrifying than having a baby. Poles were a foreign race in whom she did not have the same confidence as she did in the British or the French, although her time in Lyon had given her some reasons for lasting skepticism about the latter.

The peoples Elisabet Berg mistrusted above all others were those from the other northerly provinces, Ångermanland and Västerbotten. The former for being particularly narrow-minded, the latter for considering themselves a cut above their neighbors to the north, among whom she was obliged to count herself. She was most merciless of all towards her own kind, the people of Norrbotten, but only when they were not being compared with the other Norrland tribes.

Elisabet's greatest fear was having a defective baby. There were so many things that could go wrong. The thalidomide scandal, which had recently been playing out in the press and on television, showing pictures of children with stumps where arms and legs should have been, frightened her dreadfully. She was very scared of illness and abnormality all round, scared of the weakness they implied. It demanded a strength she did not possess.

To her relief, the boy was born healthy; Elisabet stayed at home with the baby until she went back to her job at Thule Insurance in Sveavägen, where she worked full-time. An elderly female acquaintance of Mother Svea's looked after him during the day; there were still not many day nurseries. The woman lived on Luntmakargatan, very close to where Elisabet worked, and she took the child there every morning.

The first winter it snowed so much that the snowplows could not keep up, and Elisabet struggled through the banks of snow with the pram. The boy lay in it, taking in the spectacle of the city.

He is a blank page, thought Elisabet. She had read an article about the concept of a blank page in *Dagens Nyheter*. He could be anything at all, she thought. No one knows yet.

Her son was called Erik Johansson, a name so anonymous that no one would note or remember it. Elisabet would have had no objection to something a little more distinctive, and proposed Erik Berg Johansson, but Ragnar said no. You ought not to have two surnames when one would do perfectly well. Names existed for identification and were not something to array yourself in. Wasn't she the one who generally insisted on that?

If the child had been named Erik Berg, Ragnar would have felt as though the boy was not really his, whereas giving him his father's name did not detract in the same way from his seeming to belong to his mother. For a child always belonged to its mother and was universally considered to do so. The father, on the other hand, had to compensate for the biologically weaker link by means of a stronger social link to the child through its name, something which the mother, as a consequence of how everything was arranged, could readily afford him.

People parried the state of nature with social measures to achieve a balance and give parents the incentive to do what they ought to do, thought Ragnar. It always fascinated him to discover such patterns, something that was not, however, of any interest to his wife. He wanted her to see what he saw, but it was difficult; she was not that way disposed. He had seldom encountered anyone so concrete; the firm principles which had initially impressed him proved to be not principles but feelings and opinions that were expressed as principles.

One Sunday afternoon when they were out for a walk along by the shore at Norr Mälarstrand he came to a halt in front of an advertising sign that was spinning of its own accord, even though there was barely a breath of wind. How could it be moving? He studied its construction carefully and saw that the sign was shaped like an airplane wing, which meant that it took barely any wind at all to set it off and keep it in motion.

He pointed it out, showing Elisabet what he had discovered, but it was no use. She found nothing interesting in the fact that a sign could spin by itself because it was made to follow the form and conception of an aircraft wing.

Even his thought experiments to understand how things in the world were interconnected were like unripe fruit to her, not anything she could consume. It would just fall flat when he said things like: "Imagine everybody in the world had one leg. How would bicycles look then?"

Initially he did it to show Elisabet who he was and how he worked, but she rejected it every time, taking evident satisfaction in her down-to-earth approach. Her answer was invariably of the following kind: "How could everybody in the world have one leg?"

Indeed, how could they? thought Ragnar, feeling the weight of his heart.

But she was shrewd and reliable, anyhow, and Mother Svea liked her, as did Gunnar. She had her finances in order and was never tempted into extravagance. She was immensely careful with money, Elisabet Berg, never borrowing from anyone and reproaching Ragnar if he asked his parents to help out.

Her financial probity was so complete that it got on his nerves. The fact that there was something exemplary in her thrift made matters worse. He found excellence hard to endure, especially when the possessor of that virtue was so well aware of their own excellence. If Elisabeth would just occasionally do something imprudent, like throwing out old bread or spending a hundred kronor on something she did not need, then he would have found it easier to breathe. And if only she could have dispensed with the scoffing look and unbearable self-satisfaction when she made a saving of two kronor, money he would gladly have spent for the simple joy of knowing he was not living in poverty.

Ragnar was careful with money, too, having never had that much of it to speak of, and not wasteful with what he did have. A terror of not having enough to get by on was something they had in common. But Elisabet lived as if in a permanently looming shadow of destitution. Her fear of losing everything was genuine and had rigidified into everyday practice. Sour milk was turned into little pancakes even though it gave them an acidic taste. If Ragnar pointed out that sour pancakes were not very nice, she would retort that soured foods were good for you; in Russia they lived on fermented foods and look how healthy they were. If he then objected that they weren't particularly healthy in Russia, Elisabet Berg Johansson, as she was now called, would say that if that were the case, it must be because they had stopped eating the soured Russian foods that the population had previously lived on, which had kept them as fit as fiddles.

She tripped so lightly and easily through words and thoughts. Contradictions did not worry her, and if language offered her an accessible path, she took it.

Once, when Ragnar's irritation at her economic tendencies reached such magnitude that he dared not vent it freely, he broached the topic instead with an attempt at humor:

"If you saw a ten-öre coin on the railway track just as a train was speeding towards you, would you take a chance and make a lunge for it?"

He smiled, although it took some willpower, to show that he was kindly disposed. His wife did not smile back.

"Why would there be a ten-öre coin on the railway track?"

Indeed, why would there? Ragnar again felt the weight of his heart.

Perhaps her horror of poverty stemmed from having left her family a thousand kilometers away. She was, in a way, in exile, with her parents trapped in the meager soil up there. The time Ragnar and Elisabet went to visit them, Ragnar did not understand what Elisabet's mother said, even though she was making an effort with her Swedish. She was only able to keep up the conversation with her son-in-law for an hour before asking her daughter to translate from the rustic vernacular that was her mother tongue and had no written form.

Elisabet was the only one of the siblings allowed to attend secondary school. She was expected to pay for herself, it transpired after her parents died. They had made a corresponding deduction from her inheritance.

11

I t was not stated overtly, but Ragnar knew that his wife considered those who had studied to be of a better kind. To avoid being branded as simple envy, his anger expressed itself in roundabout ways, as snaking as a river that finds its way through a landscape so that it no longer points back to its own source when it reaches the sea.

His outbursts of anger therefore seemed unfathomable and the result of some character defect; Elisabet called them moody, when in fact they were directly attributable to her.

However deeply rooted in the earth his wife was, she was also an impressively social being, flexible and able to adapt with ease to the views of the company in which she found herself. Truth was not the be-all and end-all; you had to be free to have a nice time, too.

Sociable people do not need to worry about understanding the full line of an argument: they can pretend, both to spare others and to avoid embarrassing themselves; it is the taking part that is important, the pleasure of social intercourse. Born in a different class, Elisabet had been the queen of the cocktail party, moving on from a conversation with a smile the moment it started getting more profound, but now her social life was structured in a way that precluded invitations to cocktail parties.

She had an enquiring mind, eager for knowledge, though primarily of a restricted and anecdotal kind, vivid snapshots and affirmative slogans that harmonized with the world the way she saw it.

Elisabet knew her limitations and could hear instantly if conversations were growing too abstract. She would then switch off as if others were speaking a foreign tongue that no one, least of all she herself, would expect her to follow. She left the talk to flow and thought her own thoughts in the meantime.

In this way, she could imagine that she actually understood the abstract and high-flown exchanges; it was just that the subtitles were missing. Her very presence in the room where the abstractions were being uttered showed that she was worthy. And as what is said in a foreign language in company feels a touch unreal, she could blithely break into the conversation with anything that occurred to her.

Elisabet was someone tuned to a major key. Never melancholy, gloomy, or depressive, but happy and dancing. She did not think she had the right to weigh down other people with her own state of mind or her lack of understanding of a conversation, perpetually aware as she was of belonging to the periphery of the world.

Elisabet and Ragnar were like inverted variants of one another, sometimes overlapping, sometimes antipodean.

She was receptive and liked repeating quotations of the eminent and not so eminent, from Winston Churchill and Rose Kennedy to the village idiot back home. At the same time, she claimed to loathe maxims because they were authoritarian and confining, though even that was a quotation. This borrowed antipathy for sayings of different kinds was brought home to Mother Svea whenever anything of the sort crossed her lips, which was quite frequently, because she knew her Bible. "Some feel God's punishment right away" was the most common, followed by "Pride comes before a fall." Svea pronounced these with a hint of self-distancing from such great pretensions, but this was lost on Elisabet, engrossed as she was in thoughts of how much she disliked sayings.

But if she detested sayings, thought Ragnar, why did she have so many stored away? She seemed programmed like some kind of machine to return to the sparse gardens of her memory, where nothing new was grown and nothing died.

They had been married for a year when Ragnar wondered for the first time how he was going to endure all those recurring phrases. But he would. Because once you had embarked on something, you saw it through. And to Elisabet Berg's credit it had to be said that she never sought domination through deception or cunning, only freedom for herself and others. She did not want to rule anyone, or to be ruled; did not expect to prevail over, or make decisions for, anyone but herself, and was therefore never calculating.

The combination of his insight into the necessities of existence and her mild tendency to flightiness made him shoulder the burden of family responsibility. Order and civilization were the result of a guiding hand, Ragnar knew, not an invisible one.

He found Elisabet's passivity hard to understand. It was as if she did not understand that she was in a state of interaction with other people, that they saw her, that she existed. She was competent at managing herself, but when others were involved, especially children, it was as if Elisabet did not register that it was any of her business. It was not that she was neglectful; Erik was fed and changed and content, but her relationship with the child was strange at a more subtle level, in that she felt almost as much of an outcast from the world as he was. It was impossible for her to shake off her sense of insignificance. It was so unnatural for her to instruct or to wield authority that she found it hard to see herself as a parent.

She had read a good deal, but it all went whirling round inside her, like torn-out pages without any central point for the interpretation of what had been read and the contradictions in it.

Children should be given free rein, she read, and removed the whole halter. But more than anything it was the notion of the blank page that had a distancing effect on her. If an individual was no more than what was written on that blank sheet of paper, then the world around it had an influence that was too great, and its mother a responsibility that no human being dared to carry.

Svea thought the newborn was too scrawny, with a birth weight of only two and a half kilos, and asked Elisabet if it had been a good idea to keep on with that low-fat milk during the pregnancy. She suspected Elisabet was too worried about her figure; girls wanted to look like Audrey Hepburn nowadays.

Elisabet snapped back at her, because Mother Svea's remark rekindled memories of the old grannies back home, those killjoys who had warned her against wanting to leave Norrbotten, where her old parents needed her, and against delaying marriage, with the attendant risk that it would not happen at all. And now this demand that she should drink full-fat milk, eat thick cream, and grow as plump and heavy as Mother Svea and her gang of old biddies.

But the worry that there might be something in those admonitions gnawed away at Elisabet. She read in the paper that fat was good for brain development and was afraid she had done damage to her baby by persisting with low-fat milk. Those old wives' domestic advice came from accumulated wisdom, and Elisabet did not lack respect for this ancient knowledge the way Ragnar did. He waved away all that kind of thing and said Elisabet should not listen to the old folks.

Whenever there was talk of inviting guests, he did not want his parents included. It was Elisabet who made sure that Svea and Gunnar came to visit and were on the guest list when the Johanssons were entertaining. She thought that this was what you did; in families, you belonged together. Ragnar did not share her view. He was reluctant to spoil his times of celebration and enjoyment by dragging along his old parents and being constantly under observation.

It seemed incomprehensible to him that anyone would want to draw sustenance from the steaming pile of poverty, ignorance, and impracticality that was history.

12

The chestnut on Västmannagatan was coming into bloom. Elisabet was always fascinated by its white flowers, Ragnar by the russet hue of its fruits.

But their flat was too dark, and too small now there were three of them. They had just the one room with a sleeping alcove and a kitchen, and a layout so ill-conceived that it aggravated Ragnar every time he had to spend any length of time there. It had once been the accommodation for the domestic servant of a larger, adjoining flat, but now that no normal person could conceive of being or employing a servant, the flats had been divided.

Where should they move to? That was the question.

Ragnar would have preferred a future in which he lived only in houses he had built himself, to be sure of avoiding deposits left by the past. And now that the grand state building project had been voted through Parliament, a million homes in just a few years, there was an agency dishing out site leaseholds on a first come, first served basis for self-builds in the future suburbs of Stockholm. Ragnar was in all the accommodation queues, and he joined this one, too, and was among the first names on the list.

They had been to look at a couple of flats in town, a shabby two-bedroom one on Pontonjärgatan and a dark one-bedroom place on Kocksgatan. Elisabet thought they were nice and in good locations, but Ragnar felt short of breath at the very thought of being stuck in town for the rest of his life with wheezy pipes and warped cupboard doors, where louse-infested people had crowded and coughed before him, breathing unhealthy air, in and out. He did not even consider them.

For two more years, the Johansson family stayed in their one-room flat. No offers came their way. Just when Ragnar began to fear that the only things he could give his son would be cramped living conditions, tarmac, and none of the requirements for sporting activity, a letter arrived. He had reached the top of the list for choosing a little spot to build his own house in a terrace of others at Järvafältet, an area north of the town formerly used for military exercises, where the new future would stand.

Ragnar laid out the brochure in front of them. Eighty-two houses were to be built on a slope, each half mirroring the other, otherwise identical, nothing larger nor smaller, nothing more nor less attractive than the rest, all thought through by democratic architects. Every plot owner would build his own house in accordance with the clear and un-ambiguous blueprint, with no scope for willful variation.

"It's like making a sponge cake," Ragnar told Elisabet, who baked at least one a week. "All you have to do is collect the ingredients and follow the recipe."

Spiking the cake with liqueur was not allowed, and Ragnar approved of that, for aesthetic reasons. The motley approach seldom ended up looking presentable, but it took self-discipline to refrain from it. When everybody was let loose with cans of paint and designs that they dreamt up for themselves, it was as if children had been left to their own devices: random, fun, but basically deplorable.

Every window frame, door, mailbox, doorbell, and bolt in the whole area had been planned to create a unified impression. Ragnar knew immediately that this was where he wanted to live.

But it was not quite as simple as making a sponge, he had to admit when Elisabet queried this; perhaps more like an ambrosia cake.

"You mean the one topped with glacé icing and bits of candied orange peel?"

"Yes."

Being so literal-minded and unaccustomed to metaphor, she asked: "Is that the way the roof's going to look?"

"No, the roof's made of tarred roofing felt."

"Oh, for goodness' sake, of course I know it isn't made of icing. You have to read between the lines, Ragnar. A lot of people are bad at that."

Ragnar looked down at the brochure and focused on being pleased that their plot was in such a good position, so as not to get annoyed with her.

"Maybe this is more of a Tosca cake," he said.

"With flaked almonds on the roof," put in Elisabet, and then they laughed and felt a kind of fellowship.

That very evening—it was that time of the spring when the evening light had finally returned after hesitating all winter—they took the car out of town and across the Traneberg Bridge, past Bromma airfield and out to the virgin site of the pioneering new development.

The old church helped to guide them to the right place. Elisabet was interested in historic church buildings and read in the paperwork that it dated from the thirteenth century. It would soon be surrounded by brand-new residential areas of various kinds, with a glistening town square and congruent houses all around it. Social welfare office, bank and post office, national dental service and health center, and three different food shops to promote competition.

Everything people could need would be there, and very little of what they did not. But what they merely craved rather than needed was also planned into the development, because the People's Home acknowledged individuals in all their diversity. So the shopping center would also have a state-run off-license selling intoxicating liquor and some handy park benches for the casualties of that liquor to slump on.

Other values besides commerce would shoot up and flourish here, all with the support of planning. This was not a society founded on the death of God, but a society that had wrapped itself in the mantles of gods under an omniscient power eager to get deeds done.

What, then, did people need? They needed public football fields, so all the children who wanted to play could do so. Fully lit public jogging tracks for exercise. Public swimming pools, public ice-hockey rinks and bandy fields, public libraries. Public venues where they could meet to practice the procedures of democracy and enjoy themselves at the same time.

There they could take democratic decisions to apply for more of what people needed, more meeting venues where they could gather to take further decisions about well-lit jogging tracks, sports fields, halls, rinks, pitches, and venues.

The suburb took shape at a furious pace. The smaller apartment blocks around the civic square came in modules and were put together by cranes, working alongside the builders in the mud. Two kinds of homes were created, big two-bedroom flats and big one-bedroom flats with generously proportioned kitchens with plenty of space to sit down for meals.

Nothing was crooked, lopsided, or askew. The new age was going to start here, and it was shiny and brilliant. It had taken fifty years of democracy to reach this point, five decades of dragging the old along with them as they strove for the new, and almost forty years of social democracy.

Only now had they entirely divested themselves of "back then."

Ragnar thought the new national building standards were terrific. They ensured no one would be allowed to live in hovels or rat holes ever again. True, he felt there was something rather desolate about the big apartment-block districts that surrounded their own area of houses. His sense of form sometimes collided with his belief in efficiency and a more rational future. These buildings lacked a softness, a human-facing element, but the underlying intentions were entirely good, it was a matter of urgency, and there was not an unlimited amount of money, so he decided to like what he saw.

This was his era. Without making any fuss about it, he was enthroned at its very center.

Elisabet had wanted to carry on living in the middle of town. She was someone who had been drawn to London, Berlin, Paris, and Stockholm, cities that had come so vividly to life in the novels she had read as a girl that they seemed familiar when she finally visited them; she had not left Norrbotten to end up once again in northerly exile.

They did agree, however, that children ought not to live right in the city, and by this time they had two; their daughter Elsa had just been born. So now they were off to the suburbs, where they were shortly to start building their own town house.

13

The foundations had to be laid before the frost got into the ground. Ragnar started his building project in August. He had been at work on it for four days when Mother Svea rang to say Father had died, suddenly and unexpectedly. Gunnar had collapsed in the street beside her on the way home from a coffee party in Tanto. He turned blue and convulsed. A little cluster of people formed around them. From the nearby tobacconist's, someone rang for an ambulance. Svea could do nothing to help.

Ragnar had been working on the house all day and he was tired and sweaty and was just going for a shower when the call came. He had looked forward to a rest that evening but he went straight round to Tomtebogatan.

His mother's eyes were red-rimmed but dry. The light had gone out of them. It was not just his father's life that had ended that day, Ragnar realized, but hers too. A different life lay ahead now, a distance to be covered, she was already well aware of that, had always known it, whereas Ragnar had never given the matter any thought.

Mother Svea asked if he wanted coffee. She had asked that every time he had come to visit her at home, always with affectionate solicitude for him in her voice. Even now, when everything had come crashing down around her. Yesterday had been baking day, so the battered, pastel-colored tins contained the full range of cakes and cookies.

"Where is he?" asked Ragnar.

"In cold storage at Sabbatsberg."

"Right, let's go."

"They told me I wasn't to come until tomorrow."

"But we can go there when we like! Father isn't theirs, he's ours. The hospital isn't some government department."

"We're going to do what they say. They know what's best. Won't you eat a little something, Ragnar dear? I've got pickled herring in the fridge."

Ragnar shook his head and restrained himself.

"Have you had anything to eat today? He just fell forward. It was over in a couple of seconds. I couldn't hold onto him. He hit his head."

Ragnar reached out to his mother. It was an unfamiliar feeling; he had never liked touching her and did not like it now, either. He stroked her old head with its thin, carefully combed hair, and then let his hand rest on her shoulder, though his impulse was to withdraw it when he felt the warmth of her body through the fabric of her dress.

"You mustn't blame yourself. If it was his heart, it wouldn't have helped even if you'd been able to catch him when he fell."

Ragnar thought his words sounded like someone else's. Offering solace did not come naturally to him. Life was what it was, and there was no solace to be had. Solace made him uncomfortable, it was nearly always self-deception. People deluded themselves with fabrications to help them bear the fact that there was nothing to say that would make the moment easier yet also be true.

"We always ate too much," said Svea, "that was the problem. The doctor told your father and me several years ago that we ought to lose weight. We tried over and over again, you know, but we just couldn't. We felt too hungry."

Ragnar wanted to get away from there and carry on with his life, with things that lay ahead of him. There was a house waiting to be built.

He stayed for two hours, then walked home, along by Vasa Park to the square at Odenplan, thinking how nice it felt to have escaped his parents' inconvenient and cluttered apartment, in which Svea would now have to sit all by herself. It made him shudder to think how her night would be, and all the nights to come, alone for the first time since the 1920s. It seemed incomprehensible to him that his father was dead.

The people he passed on his way looked happy and carefree. Children were playing in the park. Two hippies were in discussion with a police constable as Ragnar passed behind them. "That's your opinion, not mine," he heard one of them tell the constable before they were out of earshot.

Ragnar walked on towards Dalagatan. There were blossoms on the trees in the park. It would soon be autumn.

The building project took a break for the funeral. It was the first funeral he had attended as an adult because he loathed anything that reminded him of death and had therefore avoided all those he should have attended.

Gunnar Johansson's funeral was held in St. Matthew's Church. Afterwards there was coffee and princess gateau, the marzipan-covered confection that had been Gunnar's favorite cake. Svea wore the same black shantung-silk dress that she had worn for her mother-in-law's funeral fifteen years before, in that very same church. It was her funeral dress and she had had so little appetite in the four weeks since Gunnar died that she fit into it. She pinned on the beautiful brooch that had been a gift from her mother-in-law when she got married forty years before, and she took out the clip-on earrings that she only wore on very important occasions.

His father's death and his mother's grief brought with them obligations for Ragnar. These he discharged to the letter. He took care of all the administrative tasks, all the forms, telephone calls, and other business. Svea was immensely grateful for this, the same way she had always been grateful to Ragnar for his enormous competence.

14

After the funeral, the house building continued on weekends and after work, progressing with good speed. When Ragnar got home in the evening to the little flat that they would soon be handing back to the Housing Agency, they ate a simple dinner prepared by Elisabet. Potato cakes with bacon and lingonberries; fried potato and egg; braised ham and mustard; quiche lorraine; soup and little pancakes. Something of that kind. And they talked about how nice it would be to move into their new house.

Elisabet, who only wanted to eat food made from proper raw ingredients, always made meals from scratch and was an acolyte of chef Tore Wretman. She had been to Paris and sampled real pommes frites and could not for the life of her understand Ragnar's enthusiasm for semiprocessed products and artificial, powdered foods, especially as he had been brought up on Svea's cooking and baking.

Her literal approach prevented her from seeing that Ragnar's mania for instant foods was ideological; modern human beings had used technology to appropriate nature for their own ends, breaking down food into its component parts and re-creating them in practical sachets of powder.

Easy for quality control, light to carry home, simple to prepare, democratic.

Ragnar tried to explain, but Elisabet only half listened, not registering the extent of the thought that lay behind his words and dismissing them in her slightly unfocused way, saying you could not manipulate nature without it fighting back. To him this was a predigested, meaningless phrase born of old-fashioned, superstitious thinking.

Ragnar had seen the way Mother Svea's time was swallowed up by domestic work. The laundry that took several days, the dragging of washtubs, the long-winded heating of the water, the constant washing of dishes, the table laying, baking, and cooking. The terrible pointlessness of it all. She had to be set free from all this, which had no purpose beyond itself.

He therefore set his hopes on the new form of cookery making its entrance into the kitchens of the land. The chemists had experimented their way to every conceivable kind of tasty and nourishing food.

The powder would be the servant of mankind and the liberator of women.

As a bachelor, Ragnar had tried all the powdered foods he could get his hands on and found them phenomenal. Now, even those who could not make potato pancakes, savory cream sauce, or crema catalana could enjoy them on an everyday basis. Its powdered form also made it possible to produce perfect nutritional value. People would no longer need to be overweight, tired, and ill like Mother Svea and Gunnar.

The new instant food was a miracle transformed into a system, devised and created by human beings. Ragnar thought things were looking bright for the human race, and particularly for the Swedes, who were cutting all ties with the past.

He was as torn as a lightning-blasted pine between human creativity and necessity, the constructions of an engineering mind and the requirement for controlled acceptance of the world as it was.

Ragnar's ambivalence was also that of the People's Home, with its incompatible ambitions of fidelity to the true nature of the world and the possibility of tearing up everything that had hitherto impeded humanity.

He was at one with social democracy itself in feeling the friction between the urge to create an upwardly mobile society and the desire to help ordinary people live so well that they did not want to get away from themselves and their lot in life.

When Ragnar did the shopping, he brought home countless packs of powdered foods, even though he knew Elisabet would complain. Her aversion to throwing anything away was stronger than her desire for fresh, natural ingredients, so the sachets of powder were put to use regardless, much to her annoyance.

"Exquisite Knorr sauce, this," Ragnar would comment provocatively as they ate. "Fabulous Blue Band meat broth."

"Exquisite" was Elisabet's word, not his; she even used "delicious" and "delectable" occasionally.

On a work trip to Scotland, Elisabet bought some shortbread cookies to bring home. The packet said that they were made with real butter, making Ragnar shun them. In his view, margarine must be superior, because what went into it was created and checked by chemists in a laboratory. This fact had been confirmed by the state and the experts, because an official from the National Food Agency had recently said on the news that margarine was healthier than butter and the best choice for the Swedish people.

Elisabet did not believe it. Butter made everything taste nicer, she thought, and it was her considered opinion that natural raw ingredients must be better for the body; foodstuffs that humans had been eating since time immemorial could not be dangerous, she said. After seeing a report on television about the disgusting processes and chemicals used in the production of margarine, she never cooked with it again.

But any time Ragnar went shopping, there would be margarine in the fridge. Humanity had pulled itself up out of poverty and starvation and eradicated incurable illnesses, he explained, and none of that had been done by sitting around waiting for nature to find its own solution to the problem.

So she had to eat her Scottish shortbread herself, while Ragnar stuck to cookies from the Co-op.

The disconcerting thing about Ragnar's wife was that she, so fickle, irrational, and scornful of principles in various respects, would sometimes, by sheer intuition and down-to-earth sense, turn out more Ragnar Johansson–like than Ragnar was himself. While he, unaware of the chasm of ideas he was in, stumbled around in the rift between metaphysics and antimetaphysics, between Plato and Axel Hägerström. And both Ragnar and his carefully planned society would ultimately be torn apart by the incompatibilities, and neither of them would understand why.

How could he, hater of all artificiality, worship artificial food? Elisabet once asked him when he complained that the potato cakes had been fried in butter.

He stopped in mid-chew, set down his cutlery, and then dismissed the query, saying it was a matter of two entirely different kinds of artificiality.

One was civilization, the other was deception.

15

W hen the new Christian party was set up under the Pentecostal minister Lewi Pethrus in 1964, Ragnar warned Mother Svea not to be taken in by any talking in tongues or other aberrations. He could sense she felt tempted.

The old world lay in its death spasm, otherwise a movement like that would not need to spring up to defend the old ways, he thought, but you still did not need to throw away your vote on magic tricks. Svea did not contradict him, but took advantage of the fact that no one but God knew what a human being carried in their heart. Her pact with God was like the one Ragnar had with the state.

Yes, Ragnar was wise and clever, she thought, but also hard and angry, and there were some things he just didn't understand. She knew Ragnar judged her for feeble-mindedness, although she grasped a thing or two about life's terms and conditions that he would never understand.

In the election the autumn just after Gunnar died, Svea gave her vote to the party. A new widow did what she liked, and it couldn't be wrong to speak for Christian morals and public decency in an age of licentiousness and open petting in the park. What decided her was that children were no longer to be taught Christianity at school. She had read about it in the newspaper. Instead, they were to have something called Religious Instruction, where other doctrines would also be presented as equally right and good.

She was a gentle soul who never engaged in propaganda. Faith was such a natural thing for her that she would never have thought of doing so, but she did not like what was happening to the teaching in schools.

Svea knew that she did not observe Sundays as she ought to, so after Gunnar's death she started doing what Grandmother had said you should: abstain entirely from pleasurable domestic activities on the day of rest. No lace-making, and the loom was out of bounds. But it was hard. Time dragged. A few Sundays later she cheated and secretly spent a while at her weaving after church. When that started pricking her conscience, she decided it might be less sinful to do some sewing for the foreign mission.

The day after the general election, she told Ragnar how she had voted. He had popped round to mend a broken armchair and secure a trailing electrical cable to the baseboard so she would not trip over it.

He was dismayed, as expected, but he did not scold her; it was too late, after all, and perhaps what he wished most of all was to be rid of her, thought Mother Svea.

Instead, they talked about the Social Democrats' young new leader, only five years older than Ragnar, who had just won his first election. He seemed good, but he came from the upper classes and you could tell.

More as a scent on the air than a lucid thought, Ragnar was aware of Olof Palme ingratiating himself with the workers. It made him uneasy and on his guard. He had read that the new prime minister's wife, Mrs. Palme, had made it a condition of him taking on the responsibility that the family should have an undisturbed holiday on Fårö island every summer. The cottage they rented had no electricity or running water, which was presented as an indication of lack of pretension.

For Ragnar, it was more of a confirmation that Palme led a party in which he was a guest. Only posh people subjected themselves voluntarily to primitive living arrangements. And how impractical it was to have to take the ferry to Gotland and then another ferry to little Fårö every time they went away to the country.

When Ragnar chose his plot in Roslagen, the most important consideration was it being close to the capital and not on an island, albeit with direct access to the archipelago.

At work, however, Palme was a supporter of technical progress and a rational social structure, and that much seemed genuine. Perhaps the summers without electricity were just an unfortunate hangover from something else. And although in trying to immerse himself in the working classes, he made them out to be better than they were and better than other people, like the good-hearted aristocrat he was, an allowance had to be made for it because in the same breath he defended large-scale production and modern technology, facts and clear judgment. Ragnar found that attractive.

But he recognized the type. He was still in touch with someone about his own age whom he had met on one of his trips to Spain, even though the man felt rather alien to him, having grown up in a grand apartment on Karlavägen, with domestic servants who were not unlike Mother Svea. In the summer, when this friend took a short holiday from his job at a firm of solicitors, he wanted to live closer to nature and walk barefoot in the grass.

He presumably didn't need any servants for that, thought Ragnar, who would never dream of walking barefoot. No, it would be a case of a dry privy and an uncleaned cottage with cobwebs in the corners, furnished with castoffs.

Ragnar did not understand the urge to idealize original versions of everything, and found it hard to tolerate. To refrain from improving what could be improved was to throw away the core of humanity. On the rare occasions when he was invited to parties at such people's holiday homes, he knew what a mental endurance test it would be for him. But because you were not supposed to appear opinionated, he would go along and take part, suffer and long to be back home, feeling so bored and confined that he ate and drank too much.

The sight of revolting old kitchens turned his stomach even more than the smell of them. The others' feigned delight at the lack of electricity and running water provoked him, because it undermined the truth about those things and could be used as an excuse for leaving some people to carry on living in slum-like conditions.

He wondered whether these were matters he could discuss with his mother as he mended her armchair, but decided there was no point. She would only reply, as she always did, that she didn't understand anything any longer.

So they kept to simpler topics: the distribution of seats between the parties in the new Parliament, and Palme's performance in the final party leaders' debate before the election.

16

The society of societies appeared almost fully built. Ragnar Johansson was thirty-eight, good-looking and tall, slender and strong, with slim hips and broad shoulders, thin brown hair always kept short, and a face that seemed more carved out of solid rock with every year that passed.

In the People's Home there were many interest groups. If more than five people wanted something, they formed such a group. Sometimes they were called clubs, sometimes organizations. These could, in their turn, amalgamate into federations. The collective name for all this was *association*, the metaphysical concept *grassroots social activity*. Together they formed a *popular movement*. Popular movements were the pride and joy of Sweden.

To run a democratic association, you could get an activity grant from the taxes that were increased every year in line with what it cost to create the world's most decent society.

There were many who thought people could derive their main reason for living from grassroots activity, its meetings and exercises in democracy, its sense of community. One of the aims of "society democracy," which constituted the nerve fibers and blood vessels of the nation's body, was the chance of flexing your democratic wings. Some were more proficient at it than others, and the endless training opportunities meant they developed extremely good meeting technique; they were known as *association people.*

As these societies were bodies to which parliamentary resolutions were submitted for consideration, and were sought out by the press and broadcast media if they wanted to know the views of any particular interest group, the association people gained power in society that stood in direct proportion to their advanced meeting technique. It was not uncommon for these skills to go hand in hand with a somewhat zealous disposition and a passion for justice.

Elisabet Berg Johansson was not an association person. She was afraid of associations. Formally requesting permission to speak seemed to her an extraordinary way of conducting a conversation. In an interhuman exchange, you discussed things freely, as they occurred to you, not in the form of a contribution after you had put up your hand and been given leave to speak by a meeting leader. Waiting to speak made her so nervous that she could barely get a word out when the time came, and the procedure itself called for the contribution to be substantial enough to match the wait to be heard.

So she never asked to speak again after that time she raised her hand and waited ten minutes to be allowed to ask if the meetings could start at 7 p.m. rather than 6 p.m., so people had time to get back from work. Someone barked that this was a point of order and ought rightfully to wait for the agenda item "Any Other Business."

In the societies she belonged to—for no one escaped association life—she did not play an active part, and at annual general meetings she made herself invisible, scared as she was of being unaccountably chosen as a minutes-checker and not daring to refuse. She had no idea what a minutes-checker did, only knew that one was always appointed on a seemingly arbitrary basis by calling out a name.

Ragnar was not an association person either, but he had his love of sport. It was the backbone of the People's Home, and democratic associations were where it took place. He was thus drawn into association life and could readily see the logic in regulations and standing orders, and that it was the only fair and civilized way to reach collective decisions.

In the residential area where the Johanssons had their new house, it was not long before the Paradise Sports Association was formed. The name might have seemed surprising if you did not know it was identical to that of the district, and therefore more down-to-earth than it sounded. The association had only one section, the one for football, and only one team, for boys born in 1967. Ragnar's son Erik was born in 1967, and he was by no means the only one. Nearly all the boys in Paradise were born in 1967, and they were nearly all called Erik. The rest were called Mats, Lars, Robert, and Mikael.

Erik Johansson played as a back. Ragnar was the team trainer. His assessment, based on being a seasoned midfield strategist, was that Erik would be best in defense.

At a meeting of the newly formed Paradise Sports Association, he volunteered for the task of designing the players' uniforms. For this he took inspiration from the kit worn by the Dynamo Moscow team at the end of the 1940s, particularly the shorts. He had been to see Dynamo play at the Råsunda Stadium in Solna in October 1947, when they were on their propaganda tour around Europe. What play, and what unforgettable shorts!

The morning after that match, he had propped a photograph from *Dagens Nyheter* in front of Mother Svea's sewing machine and asked her to make him a pair. That very afternoon, Svea went into Stockholm, to Paul U. Bergström's by the Hötorget flower market, and bought some durable white cotton fabric and a sewing pattern, which she then modified herself. Neither before nor since had she seen her son so happy. He proudly wore his wide Dynamo shorts to every practice session until he grew out of them.

Ragnar also designed Paradise FC's tracksuits and club badge. In the newly formed association in the newly built residential area, they had decided unanimously that the club colors would be yellow and blue.

By the very next meeting, Ragnar had his design ready: it had a purity and simplicity of line but was also soft and comfortable. The capacious shorts were a single color, cornflower blue, and reached almost to the knee; the shirt was blue, with a bright-yellow stripe running from shoulder to hem. No yellow on the cuffs, the socks the same color as the shorts, no superfluous fancy touches, and the club badge sewn on the left-hand side of the chest.

Paradise FC's seven-man team of nine-year-old boys practiced twice a week and played a match once a week against other teams in the district. Ragnar did not betray by a single word or look that he could see which boys would come to something on a football field, nor that his son was among the better players on the team. He gave the same short, efficient commands to everyone, and only gave praise when there was good reason, and on the basis of exceeding expectations; the good players received no praise for doing something that earned their less-agile teammates an encouraging word.

The practice sessions were always held on the generous stretches of green space provided for outdoor activity below the rows of houses in Paradise. In a well-worn tracksuit and with an occasional blast on his whistle, Ragnar followed the action on the field with a look of intense concentration.

His daughter Elsa stood beside him, her gaze just as concentrated but focusing on other things that were at her own height. When she asked why one of the team often stood behind another player so no one could pass to him, Ragnar explained without taking his eyes off the game that the boy was scared of the ball. How could you be scared of a ball? she asked.

"You can if you're afraid of making a mistake."

"So why does he play football then?"

"For the comradeship," said Ragnar, squinting out across the pitch so that the laughter lines appeared at the corners of his watchful eyes like little fans opening out.

"The comradeship is the important part."

17

They were wonderful years. For Sweden. For Ragnar and Elisabet Johansson. They had permanent jobs and security. They paid their bills on time, got on well, and did not drink. Elisabet dreamed, though not that intensely, of winning money, and bought a lottery ticket on the second of every month. Her birthday was September 2, and she therefore thought of two as her lucky number, which her husband sometimes laughed at, sometimes sighed over.

The country had sped like a javelin through the sixties, and by the seventies it was near the top of every list of national comparisons. It had the most day care places, the lowest income disparity, the greatest film director, the foremost children's writer, the best slalom skier, tennis player, and pop group, the most impressive gender equality, the highest taxes—all of them sources of real pride.

What was more, the country had a prime minister who was greater than his country and too intelligent for it, and a party that was so extraordinarily good for the majority of people and efficient for the country's large-scale industry that it was never voted out, even though there had been universal suffrage and equal votes for women since 1921. And to that could be added countryside so beautiful that no one thought about how ordinary it was.

The better things went for Sweden and the Johansson family, the more moans and complaints were heard from people on the left and on the right, the ethereal, disembodied beings and the spoilt crew who had lost their domestic servants.

When Ragnar had his long summer holidays and Elisabet was at work at her insurance company, Mother Svea would be with him and the children out at the cabin for weeks at a time, making the meals and baking the cakes and cookies for dunking in the coffee. The children had the benefit of sunshine, council-run swimming lessons, and boat trips in the new plastic gig that Ragnar had bought on the west coast, towed home on a trailer, and fitted out in shining, varnished mahogany. Elisabet joined them for the workplace holidays in July.

Ragnar was hardly ever bothered by enforced idleness and depression now that he had the children. They would set out nets together, and Erik drove the boat while Ragnar hauled in the nets. He shouted his orders so loudly that they could be heard all over the bay—Back! Forward! Neutral!—and as if it were a matter of life and death to pull up the cod, bullhead, and perch caught in the net overnight. When Svea told him he sounded too angry and was scaring the children, Ragnar replied that it wasn't a question of anger but of clarity. On the water, instructions had to be distinct.

He taught the children to ride bikes and showed them how to gut fish. He often gave them little pedagogical problems to solve so they would learn to think and to see the world clearly.

"What weighs most," he would ask, "a kilo of cotton or a kilo of lead?"

Upon which Elsa would triumphantly and unreflectingly exclaim that of course a kilo of lead weighed more.

Perhaps she was not really all that bright, thought Ragnar, but no matter, because he was committed to a society where even the slower-witted would have a place.

Yes, those were good years.

On Swedish Radio, an engineer of the People's Home said that ideally any community should be built so that its citizens were only a cycle ride or a walk from where they worked. No one should have to sit in their car in a traffic jam morning and evening, or endure long, crowded commutes on public transport. This was an atrocious waste of productive time that could be put to better use.

When he moved to Paradise, Ragnar had already applied for a job at one of the new secondary schools nearby and been offered it. Elisabet's office had moved from central Stockholm to Solna, so she was able to cycle to work.

Another engineer of the People's Home said on Swedish Television that if the Swedish people wanted to show greater solidarity with the social project, they ought to stop baking and making jams and fruit juices at home, as this was to be considered a form of tax evasion. The state needed all the value-added tax it could bring in to create and pay for a good life for everyone, just as it needed the tax income that would have accrued if those hours of domestic work had been devoted to paid employment instead.

When he heard this, Ragnar thought of his perpetually baking, jam-producing, juice-making mother: he had been right in his passion for instant foods and large-scale production, and in his vision of her as an ancient monument from the agrarian age. In modern-day life, self-sufficient households would not do.

18

The purpose-built suburb—although there was some dispute as to the exact nature of that purpose—had existed for six years. People from every province of Sweden had flocked there and then moved on. The flats were the most spacious, light, and modern in the whole country, but notwithstanding that, their occupants quit them in a steady stream, as soon as they had the opportunity. The original incomers from Småland, Finland, and Norrland were replaced by political asylum-seekers from Valparaiso and Diyarbakir, and economic migrants from Kulu and Thessaloniki. People came from the repressive circles of the juntas to a land where Svea Johansson went to a sewing circle every Tuesday.

The team of teachers at Ragnar's school saw alienation and trouble arriving in the wake of this change. They were all in agreement that the responsibility for sounding the alarm lay with those who encountered the problem first; it was up to them to alert the representatives of democracy, so the problem could be addressed before it was too late. Swedish democracy was built on nothing else but science and pragmatic correction on the basis of empirical observation, not on unshakable principles of an unverifiable metaphysical nature. Politicians therefore needed the help of citizens and professionals to find out what reality looked like, so they could use this knowledge to reshape things in the best interests of each and every individual.

The teaching staff decided to write an official letter to the Stockholm City politicians about the situation in the new suburb.

Ragnar's view of the matter was clear, and he had thought it through. Big concentrations of newcomers from other countries in the same place had a different impact on the area as a whole than a series of individuals did.

How these immigrants to Sweden were treated was something that would have crucial repercussions, wrote the staff, and that was why it was vital to get it right from the outset. They could not possibly put all the immigrants in the same location; such places would deviate too much from the rest of the country. Their local population was already made up of thirty percent immigrants, and numbers were constantly on the rise; the proportion could hardly go any higher without far-reaching and unpredictable consequences.

They wrote that it was impossible to provide a proper standard of teaching in classrooms where the children of the illiterate were to be given the same opportunities for attainment in school as the children whose parents had lived on Swedish soil for centuries, with shared customs and elementary schooling for all, for the past one hundred thirty years. They wrote that these children should not be made to suffer for the sake of adults' politicking.

The official letter was completed. Before it was sent off, to be on the safe side, Ragnar wanted to show it to the principal, a man in whom he had the utmost confidence. During his lunch break, he went to the principal's office and knocked on the door.

The principal, Erland Borgström, was an elderly man, classically educated, who wore a tweed suit and waistcoat and had always lived alone. He liked going to the opera but had never attended a football match, was as happy reading the classics as newly published books, could not tell the difference between a jointer plane and a handsaw, but got on exceptionally well with Ragnar Johansson. On many occasions he had shown his particular trust of Ragnar's judgment and competence.

Ragnar asked him to read the letter and see if there was anything to find fault with.

They sat in the corner of the room the principal kept for visitors, with two wing chairs and a low table made of pear wood between them. Ragnar waited while the principal read the letter. The school was on a hill, so the view was quite good, even though there was not much to have a view of in that part of town.

Erland Borgström put down the letter, stretched his short, stocky body, which had never been subjected to any physical exertion, and placidly filled his pipe. With the jovial, distanced perspective on life that self-confidence confers, the principal never let himself be hurried. He went through a complicated pipe-lighting procedure and puffed away for a good while before answering Ragnar's question. But Ragnar was not impatient or apprehensive in Erland Borgström's presence; he knew that when the answer came it would be honest and carry weight.

"The fault one might perhaps find is that what you and your colleagues express here could have been said in similar terms by a group of business magnates in leafy Djursholm fifty years ago."

Ragnar asked what the principal meant.

"On the outbreak of democracy, or just after, when its effects were dawning on each and every one of them."

Erland Borgström relit his pipe and let his eyes rest on the view, but never for one moment lost sight of Ragnar's agitation or the set of his jaw.

"But mark well, Ragnar, and you if anyone will understand what I'm saying here: it might be the right thing, even so, providing the letter is necessary and in full accordance with the truth. Which I assume it is?"

"The situation is serious. A large part of each lesson is spent trying to keep order in the classroom. There isn't much time left for teaching."

"That is naturally not desirable."

"But what do you mean when you say it could have been written by magnates in Djursholm fifty years ago?"

With the stem of his pipe, Erland Borgström indicated the letter on the table between them.

"The worry that children of unschooled parents will be taught in the same establishments as the children of people who have been educated for generations, for no other reason than that there will be disruption and a decline in teaching standards in schools."

Ragnar thought about this. Conscious as he was of the principal's rock-solid support for his own person, he was able to think clearly even though he was under duress.

"I don't see it as the same thing."

The principal was still looking out over the railway, which divided the new and troubled suburb from the older, more tranquil settlement, where families had lived in the same house for decades, after which their children would live there for decades more.

"In what respect is it different?"

"Our letter only says the new arrivals in Sweden need to be spread around in different locations by means of central planning. The people with the overview are surely the ones who have to take responsibility for those decisions? Not individuals. Individuals will naturally do what seems most favorable for them at that moment."

The principal's pipe had gone out, and he busied himself with lighting it again.

"Your belief in social planning is a very potent one, Ragnar. More potent than mine. I have to admit I'm a little frightened of it, actually."

"There's nothing to be frightened of."

"Oh, I think there is. You know water finds its way through whether we want it to, or not. It will run wherever it finds a channel. Was it Willy Kyrklund who wrote a short story about that, or was it Sven Delblanc? I can't remember now."

"If you drain and build channels and pipes, water runs where you want it to run. Nature needs a helping hand. It won't do anything for humans of its own accord, humans have to organize it themselves, tame nature to make it serve them. Isn't that what civilization is?"

"Or civilization is understanding when you need to take a step back from your blind faith in yourself and your ability to plan for everybody else."

They sat in silence, each ruminating on their own thoughts. Then Ragnar said: "Do you think we're going to have problems?"

Ragnar took the letter and put it back in its envelope.

"I do. But nothing that can't be handled. I know you well enough, Ragnar, to be aware you don't look down on people for their origins."

The principal was largely right on that score. What Ragnar looked down on was irrationality. It was a matter of regret and pity to him how far irrational cultures still had to go, because they, like everybody else, could only take one step at a time. Every time his wife said how refined the English were compared to the uncouth Swedes, with their rustic ways, Ragnar reminded her of their idiotic lack of central heating and their hopeless windows that opened upwards instead of outwards.

The letter was duly sent.

A month later, a reply arrived from the city representatives. In this it was made clear that they took a very dim view of the teachers' letter, which spoke ill of people whom the country of Sweden badly needed, who had fled for their lives from danger, persecution, and war, people bringing with them so many good qualities that would be useful to Sweden, and from whom the unbending Swedes had a lot to learn. The teachers were warned against adopting such a xenophobic tone.

Ragnar felt affronted by the reply, but also dumbfounded. Its logic was beyond comprehension. The teachers' proposal had been for the authorities to place incomers from faraway cultures in locations where they would be most beneficial to Swedish society. For those who had escaped persecution and poverty, he said once he had read the city's response several times, the most important factor was surely not being allowed to choose the place where they would live, in a country where they had no link to any place whatsoever? Wasn't that self-evident?

He went quiet, merely muttering as he followed without comment the progress of the latest distant war and its direct impact on his daily working life.

Then he went to see Mr. Borgström again. The room smelled of sweat, aftershave, and pipe tobacco. Ragnar was feeling dejected. He needed the principal's corroboration of his stance towards haughty politicians.

"But wasn't this more or less what we predicted?" said Borgström.

"Not me. Because this is no answer. They don't address any of our concerns, but just tell us what they think is wrong with us."

"That's rhetoric, Ragnar. Politics is rhetoric. It always has been, and always will be."

Ragnar did not know exactly what rhetoric was, not to the extent that he could have explained it to someone who asked him, and that was the hallmark of true knowledge.

"Rhetoric dupes us with words," said Borgström, as if he had read Ragnar's thoughts. "It doesn't seek the truth, but sells it for easy applause, for an elegant lie, a straying path through a beautiful landscape. Plato was the first person to point to it, so it dates back a long way."

Ragnar's dejection failed to lift. He wondered how you amassed such learning as Erland Borgström possessed, and thought that it was not for him. Besides, it was too late.

———

While others moved from the new suburb, the Johanssons stayed put. Elisabet wanted them to move before Elsa started school, and raised the topic at least once a year. Growing up on the periphery had honed her sensibility to various matters. She instinctively understood that it was not good for children to live in a place everyone abandoned as soon as they could. The signs were all too familiar to her.

Every time Elisabet said they ought to move for the sake of the children, Ragnar said he had no trouble seeing through her bourgeois aspiration to have people beneath her.

"This place serves us and our children very well."

And that was the end of the conversation.

His real argument was a different one. It was to do with the moment of truth, with standing your ground when the bull charged. He only once put that argument into words, and then in his deepest tone of voice, the one he used when the knowledge he imparted was settled and incontrovertible.

"Anyone who copes with attending these schools," he said, "can cope with anything."

He was prepared to protect Erik and Elsa with his life, but lulling them into a false sense of security was not taking care of them. They had to be made ready for friction. Children were to be shaped by realities, not by false comfort. He did not intend to fail his children or the concept of Swedish society by moving somewhere more select as soon as any resistance presented itself.

There was another reason for staying in the purpose-built suburb, surrounded by large areas of green.

"Where else in a big city," he said in the same deep tone, "could children and young people have such unsurpassed access to sport?"

Where, if not in the forest setting of the suburb, with space for all manner of health-promoting activities?

19

I t was important for Ragnar Johansson that his children should not be obliged to do the same thing as he had. Sport was a must, they had no choice on that point, for without sport, life lacked meaning and structure, but the disciplines that had been his would not necessarily need to be theirs. The issue did not arise for Elsa anyway, because girls did not play ice hockey, and their football was at a deplorably low level.

With a firm hand, Ragnar steered his children towards individual sports. The duty to see the whole picture and what was best for the team had an obverse side, which had been brought home to him by his own experience of life: not everyone was dutiful; some were happy to let others do the hard work. If his children were to be part of a team, how far they could go would depend on others, whereas he wanted it to lie in their own hands, and thus also in his.

This was one of his reasons for buying Erik a racing bike and enrolling him in a cycling club. The more immediate reason was Bernt Johansson's Olympic gold in Montreal in 1976.

When Ragnar was sixteen, Harry Snell's world championship title made him want to be a competitive cyclist, and he had entered a race and won it. It was a twenty-kilometer pursuit from Karlberg Palace through Huvudsta, around Jungfrudansen and back, and he did it on a heavy military bicycle. He had neither the equipment nor the support for individual sports, and for that reason he had not carried on with it. He therefore promised himself that his children would never lack either equipment or backup.

The triumphs of Björn Borg did not appreciably influence Ragnar or Erik; tennis was alien to them, and they did not watch the broadcasts from Wimbledon unless they happened to be sitting in front of the television. Nor could it have been downhill skiing, despite Ingemar Stenmark. As a dyed-in-the-wool Stockholmer, he felt the concept of downhill skiing to be as far removed from him as tennis. Storlien and the Alps lay in a world that was not his.

The year Erik turned eleven, he started competing in cycle road races. The Johansson family would travel to competitions every weekend from early April to late September, first round the Mälaren Valley, then Bergslagen and central Sweden, then the whole country.

The Paradise seven-a-side team was disbanded, and there was not much left of the Sports Association; it stood or fell with Ragnar. He was now wholly focused on learning the strict norms and codes of cycling, how to mend tires and straighten out bent wheels.

Weekend after weekend, the family left home early and got back late, or stayed over in cheap hostels. Elisabet would rather have stayed at home and slept in after her week at work. But then she would never have seen her husband and children on Saturdays or Sundays.

Sport took over family life. Little else was spoken of, or planned for. Discussion was of names and results, times, average speeds, and training techniques. TV viewing revolved round sports programs; all disposable income went on equipment, petrol, and accommodation.

Elisabet was constantly cooking starchy meals, baking bread, washing training gear, mending burst seams, sewing on sponsor logos, and preparing packed lunches for the next competition trip.

She longed to get back to reading books and socializing with friends over food and drink on weekends like other people did, going to the cinema and theater, not spending her time in parochial little places without a single traffic light. She remembered a time when she had been an autonomous adult individual, who took care of herself and enjoyed what the big city had to offer. But sport reduced her to a service provider.

She told Ragnar it would be nice to go on holiday occasionally, to places with plenty of culture and history; to be in the company of friends they had chosen themselves, in places other than the side of the road. Ragnar derived no enjoyment from that sort of thing; it was a craving for amusement and pointless relaxation with no purpose beyond pure experience. The only trips he wanted to make were ones with direction and meaning, that is, those journeys round Sweden to training camps and competitions, where his children benefited from pitting their strength against others and being part of the distinguished community of sport, as he sometimes put it.

Ragnar had found something crucial to live for.

Like Ragnar, Erik had natural physical strength and proved to be an instinctive tactician in the peloton. In virtually every race in the years that followed, he was in contention. On the rare occasions when he gave up a hundred meters before the finish line and fell back to the rear of the field, having judged that he would not come in the top few places, Ragnar rebuked him long and hard in the car on the way home, or sat in icy silence until the eventual outburst a couple of days later.

The laxity of not doing your best at every moment was what Ragnar could not tolerate, because it frightened him. If one did not always do one's best, the next step could be losing control of one's entire life and falling into the gutter, losing everything. Trying to decide at every moment how much effort to put in was impossible. That sort of fine-tuned, all-seeing sensitivity was beyond human capability. So there was only one way forward: to follow a principle and an agreed-on plan and not to deviate from it. You gave your all when competing. You did not rely on transitory feelings.

Laziness and the longing to make things easy were so infernally insidious that they disguised themselves as good judgment and tricked people into not exerting themselves.

Having discharged his wrath by communicating this philosophy and determination, he would add that every participant in a sporting competition was under an obligation to show respect for the concept of sport and for their fellow competitors by not being nonchalant.

Erik never replied to these onslaughts. He held his tongue and submitted to them. Ragnar saw the resentment growing in him, but did not think he himself could act any differently; it was his fundamental responsibility to show his children what life was all about.

Erik had most things, but he lacked drive. He seemed to be permanently measuring out an internal distance between himself and the world, a space that also protected him from his father's didactic program. Erik was evasive, and evasion is the most intractable obstacle to an ambition to achieve.

Girls' sporting activities were a decidedly hazier area for Ragnar than the boys' equivalent. Women's sport was underdeveloped, and he was unsure what Elsa should go in for. There were always the classic disciplines, of course, the ones the Greeks engaged in, or would have done if Greece had had snow in winter.

He liked the natural branches of sport that were self-explanatory and had not been invented at a desk, branches that would spontaneously reappear if all human memory were wiped clean. Human beings had their nature and their natural behavior. Contrivances could not compete, or at least never became more than peripheral phenomena. Time ground away anything too convoluted. People could con themselves with artificialities for a short period, but events that entailed jumping fifty meters on one leg, or running the hundred meter backwards, did not last. People wanted to understand what was being tested, thought Ragnar, what they knew had been established when a winner was acclaimed. An event needed an inner logic if it was not to become pointless and uninteresting.

Sport was what would save his daughter from the wretched female fate that awaited her if she did not receive the right guidance in time. He must give her access to something more impressive than passivity and staring into the mirror. In sport, with its clear goals—victories and constant improvement—there was no room for worrying about broken fingernails and runs in her tights. It encouraged not weakness but strength, and not the special repertoire of helplessness and cunning, in that explosive combination that was women's undoing.

Elsa would devote herself to one of the solid branches of sport, in which women started on a level footing with men. There were three possible options. Running, skiing, and swimming. In the case of running, Wilma Rudolph with her wonderful steps could serve as inspiration, if Elsa needed role models of her own sex, although he doubted it, strongly and as a matter of principle. In the case of skiing, she would have Toini Gustafsson and the Russian women.

Cross-country skiing was a venerable branch of the sport, with Nordic ancestry and no frills. Elisabet wanted her to take ballet lessons, because they made you graceful and gave you good posture, but Ragnar forbade it. Ballet was for a different sort of people.

He enrolled Elsa in a skiing club. It soon became clear to him that she possessed the most important quality for success in sport, namely the ability to concentrate. She was never absent-minded or preoccupied, always focused straight ahead, on the next training session, the next race and its finish-line banner. She had inherited that from him, he thought, the concentration. And the tongue pro-truding between her teeth when she was really intent on something.

Over her first two seasons, Elsa was unbeaten, and Ragnar felt a quiet happiness. Life had once again taken a richer turn.

The traveling and competing now extended across the whole year, and even his sense of gloom at the prospect of the winter darkness was pushed aside. He learned to wax skis and soon knew all there was to know about course conditions in temperatures from minus seventeen to plus five. With his uncommon understanding of materials and the regularity of phenomena, he understood the essential nature of waxing more quickly than most beginners. In the seasons that followed, he made not a single waxing miscalculation that put Elsa out of contention, not even when the going was most sticky and difficult.

From October to April, he and Elsa paid careful attention to the snow charts to help with the planning of training sessions and competitions. Their perpetual hope for precipitation and temperatures below freezing in Stockholm in winter lent a whole new gravity to the weather forecast.

Elisabet now had even less scope for her own interests. But Ragnar was thinking not of her but of the fact that he was doing something of crucial importance for his children, while the nagging sensation that life was an empty vessel in which you were trapped and then died was dulled by the vitality of sport and his children's successes.

He lived in a kind of rapture, but the operation required so much work, discipline, and tension that it was only afterwards he realized it had been happiness, the only happiness he found worthy of the term, because it set its sights on refining and improvement.

Notwithstanding her powers of concentration, Ragnar's daughter made the most bewildering mistakes. Sometimes he wondered if she was deficient in some way, so baffling were her misjudgments. When she attempted to make her first sponge cake using an instant cake mix to which she only had to add water, she read on the packet that a deciliter and a half of water should be added to the sachet of powder. She took a swift and headstrong decision that this was too little water for a whole sponge cake, and that it must mean a liter and a half. Elsa poured that amount of water onto the powder, most of which stayed in lumps, floating and not dissolving. Ragnar came into the kitchen to see how things were progressing with the cake to have with his coffee.

"What's this?"

"It's the cake mix."

"But it hasn't mixed in properly."

"No, there's too much water."

She explained her thinking.

"Why would you assume the instructions on the packet are wrong?" he asked, making an effort to gain some understanding of the way she thought, which often seemed to him most odd and worrying.

"You can't start out by questioning the recipe, Elsa. It isn't likely to be wrong. And you can't just decide for yourself how much water the cake needs."

He recognized her embarrassment, his own companion of former days, which was now coloring her cheeks and neck. But she also looked thoughtful.

"I don't understand how a deciliter and a half of water can be enough for a whole sponge cake."

"You don't need to understand it. Let those who know about this make the decisions and just follow the recipe."

"I thought it seemed far too little water."

"So you multiplied it by ten."

"Is there anything between deciliters and liters?"

"What do you mean?"

"I don't know."

He poured the mixture down the sink and took a packet of shop-bought cookies out of the larder to have instead.

"Thinking is good, Elsa, of course. But doing it right is better still."

"I thought I *was* doing it right."

"What do you imagine it would do to their sales if they gave the wrong instructions on the packet?"

"But they must get it wrong sometimes, surely?"

"Hardly ever."

"But even if it only happens once, someone's got to be the person who discovers it?"

"And you should be very wary of believing it's going to be you."

Their conversations made him vaguely uneasy; there had been no exchanges of this kind with his son. Erik was more at one with the world, more comfortable in it. At the parents' meetings at Elsa's nursery when she was younger, he never asked if she was coping well or making progress, but whether she had any friends. Erik had lots and never had any problem making new ones, but sullen types like her found it harder, in his experience. Friends were confirmation of your acceptance by others, thought Ragnar, and people had to behave in a way that made them acceptable. Societies would be impossible otherwise, and individual lives too heavy.

20

When the football World Cup was staged in Argentina under the rule of the military junta, and they had watched a report about it on television, Elsa asked why the Argentinian players were not allowed to have long hair. Ragnar, who found the rule entirely reasonable, explained to her that it was very impractical playing football with long hair, but it was also scruffy and pointed to undesirable character traits in that player: preoccupation with himself rather than with his team or his country.

"The players don't represent themselves. You hardly ever represent yourself, and even if you don't feel as though you're representing something or someone else, others will understand that you are."

Elsa listened intently, as she always did when her father spoke.

"So who do *I* represent, then?"

"You're a blank page," said Elisabet.

"If you're abroad, you represent Sweden," said Ragnar. "If you're up in Norrland, you represent Stockholm; if you're over in the shopping center, you represent Paradise. And here in Paradise, you represent the Johansson

135

family. People's connections are determined by fixed structures. Things aren't free-floating, and it's not up to you to decide."

"Paradise is an oasis," said Elisabet, whose mind was on the television and a series she was watching.

She often called Paradise an oasis, but just then, neither Elsa nor Ragnar thought it was relevant to the subject at hand. Elsa concentrated on the subject, because it presented her with a lot to think about.

Elisabet had previously given her children information that directly contradicted Elsa's father's words, telling them that they should never be ashamed of other people; this was on some occasion when the children were ashamed of something Elisabet had said or done. Elsa had felt there was something odd about her mother's assertion, and now found it did not tally at all with what her father said about always representing someone or something else. Every child knew you were supposed to feel a sense of shame when your parents did something that made you cringe. It was completely obvious to everyone that offspring could not be free of their parents. So what did her mother mean?

The subject of the Argentinian team had produced a lot of strange notions for Ragnar's daughter to grapple with. The question of how the length of a person's hair could indicate their character, for example. Ragnar had no answer to that, although he was in no doubt that this was as he said it was, even though he could offer no evidence.

———

There were many new theories of child-rearing in circulation at that time. Sweden was the country of children, and the new and better world had to start with them. The aim of all these theories was to reject what had gone before, because history was a dead hand of human ignorance. It was an attitude with which Ragnar should have sympathized, but instead his blood began to boil every time he found himself in conversation with other parents, usually the mothers of his children's friends. Ragnar, born in the 1940s, had come late to fatherhood, and they were all at least ten years younger than him. They looked as if they wanted to overthrow the social democratic model for society, with clothes in vegetable-dye colors, round glasses, and bags made of untanned leather. Their children called them by their first names, and the mothers declared that children knew better than their parents, and definitely knew enough to decide things for themselves. Your job as a parent was to be on hand as a friend and a resource but not to try to direct, because who could claim that adults knew anything about kids that they didn't know better themselves?

Elisabet and Ragnar never used the term *kids*. It seemed to them to be a word used by other, more casual kinds of people who drew no distinction between humans and the natural world. The Johansson family was an exceedingly animal-free zone. Only Mother Svea understood animals and cared about them.

When Ragnar listened to the mothers, his blood rose above the boiling point, hissing and spitting, frying him from the inside.

"The only thing is," he said through clenched teeth, "that if you ask children what they want to do, they don't know."

Was he also not supposed to pass on knowledge to his pupils, knowledge he had acquired over half a lifetime, but to look on in feigned equality of merit and let them run riot with hammers, nails, and saws among the pieces of wood? Was he supposed to tell them that there were no harmonies to strive for, that all forms were as good as each other, because perfection and harmony were illusions invented by other people as tools of oppression?

He expected the other parents to strike back. The women around him should have found it maddening, but their only reaction was a slight nervousness in the face of this sharper tone, an uneasiness mainly evident in the way it transmitted itself to the many items of jewelry round their wrists and necks. And then they changed the subject.

They all seemed to have bought their phrases in multi-packs at bargain prices, while he had chiseled out his own with great care to produce something as truthful and genuine as it was within his power to achieve. They did not care whether what they said was correct, as long as they said something.

That was how it seemed to him.

When nobody in the group reacted to his words, he repeated what he had said, more slowly and emphatically.

"If you ask children what they want, they don't know. That's why you have to guide them, so they can find out what they want to do one day."

But then someone did speak up and contradict him. She was the mother of a girl in Elsa's training group, an unassuming girl who turned up at training when she felt like it, meaning the rest of them had to wait for her on the brow of the hill. That was what happened when you didn't pull your weight, thought Ragnar: you made demands of other people and wasted their time. But this girl's mother never seemed concerned that her daughter was bringing down the whole group by being worse than the rest of them. And she had turned out that way, Ragnar presumed, because she was allowed to do whatever she felt like doing at the time, instead of what promoted her own ability.

Her mother was a librarian in Sundbyberg, and told Ragnar that he was giving expression to an unpleasant view of people, and a view of children that went against all research. Children knew very well what they wanted, and it was seldom the same as what their parents wanted, but because the children were dependent on their parents, and loyal to them, they tried to want what their parents wanted so as not to perish.

Ragnar sensed something insinuating in her tone that caused the old shame and anger, against which he was completely defenseless, to invade his body.

"Research!" he snapped. "What sort of research is that? Do you mean they've got a machine that can see into children's brains and read what they're really thinking? Finding answers to questions like that is as impossible as researching whether the chicken or the egg came first, surely? The experts will no doubt reach the conclusions they'd already decided on."

The woman thought about what he had said without getting worked up about his opposition. The fact that she took his words seriously surprised him so much that his indignation abated.

When she had finished thinking, she said: "You could have a point there. It isn't a question of research, you're right, but more of an outlook on life. But you seem to start from the assumption that a human being is born a blank, and can, and ought to be, molded. It's a pet idea of liberals, that we can direct the world ourselves. But we're not born blanks, we're programmed. Most things are laid down in us. I think so, anyway. And on top of that come all our experiences, which we deal with according to the way we are, not the other way round. It's not the experiences that make us the way we are, but how we already are that decides how we handle them. Or so I believe, because you're right that it isn't an empirical question but a basic assumption, a postulation. We're almost complete at birth, that's what I think."

He eyed the librarian intently as he attempted to follow what she said. *Postulation* and *empirical questions* were unfamiliar concepts, but not even that put him off. He hadn't had the faintest idea that he embraced liberal pet ideas. How had that happened? He definitely wasn't a liberal. If he had inadvertently nurtured notions of that kind, why then his whole construction could be wrong.

He pulled himself together to ask a question. It was about whether, in that case, you could in any way direct how a human being was formed. He was so interested in the subject at issue that he was not the least bit acerbic, nor defensive in any other way.

The woman smoothed down her impeccably groomed, center-parted, dark-blonde hair.

"These are questions that are too difficult for me," she said. "I took an anthropology option at university, and I've read some Chomsky for my own interest, but that's all."

"Who?"

"The theoretical linguist. American."

The woman waited for him to say something.

"But if you want to know what I think," she went on when Ragnar remained silent, "it's that nurture has a marginal influence, but not as much as people believe. And that parenthood is about shaping a harmonious, independent individual. And I think you do that by giving the child the preconditions for learning to live with the nature they've been born with."

Ragnar fixed her with a look that his fervent concentration made even more vividly blue.

"How do you shape an individual like that?"

"If only I knew. But I generally say that most children look after their parents, not the other way round."

And your child is the exception that proves the rule, of course, he thought, irritated afresh, but mostly by the vastness of his own lack of knowledge.

What attitude should he adopt to these things? Was it the case that the indistinct contours of the librarian's daughter could not have been made firmer and more precise, even with him as her guide? Would the result remain loose and listless because her constitution was loose and listless, whereas something else entirely would come of his own daughter's efforts because she was already the way he wanted to make her?

In that case, his disciplinarian exercises were unnecessary, his outbursts meaningless, beyond creating discord and unpleasantness in the family, and his worries about his children's requirement for guidance and shaping equally so. Perhaps everything was already determined within their bodies and psyches.

It struck him that what the woman said matched the way he already saw the world. It was an outlook that meant Ragnar could only tolerate the idea of the chosen few in the context of top athletes. Bodies could be trained and honed, while the intellect appeared to him unamenable to change through diligence. Mental capacity seemed to him given, fixed in its position, whereas the body was raw material that could be refined until its fullest perfection had been reached. In all other respects, you were who you were.

He had to find out where the truth lay in all this. Where could he turn? Building a chimney was simple enough to learn from an instruction manual, but what kind of books should he seek out for this? Books on the subject of whether a person *is* or *comes into being*? What could have been written about that?

The librarian might know; she had mentioned one name he had already forgotten. But he did not want to invest her with unlimited power just because she had said something he would probably never forget.

21

One Saturday morning in November when Elsa was ten, and approaching her third season still unbeaten in competitive events, she and Ragnar drove the barely five kilometers to the golf course in Järfälla for one of their regular training sessions.

The first snow had fallen. It lay in a thin layer on the mown grass of the golf course. The air temperature was around zero, and the sleety snow beat against their faces like sharp tacks. The exercise track was green and skiddy.

Ragnar could see his daughter's distaste and was aware of his own reluctance to venture out in this weather, but he thought that it was at moments like this she must be able to resist convenience, and he his sympathy for her.

"Ugh, what horrible weather," said Elsa as they were parking. "It's not going to be very nice on the track today."

She got out of the car, holding up her arm to shield her face from the sharp snow particles. He had never seen her so unfocused and unwilling before a training session. The awful thing about it was the presentiment it gave him of a day when she might turn her back on what was fundamental, and he would have no way of stopping her.

As they stood there, each of them despondent for their separate reasons, a skier came by, someone they recognized. He was keeping up a challenging pace, and his ski suit had salty deposits striped across the lower back; he must have been skiing since before dawn. The man gave them a brief nod and fought on, head down, face set into a grimace. His name was Jyrki Ristolainen, and he had come fifth in the big Vasaloppet race back in March. Two years earlier he had resigned from his job on the production line at the Marabou chocolate factory in Sundbyberg and started work as a garbage collector so he would have more time to practice, even though he was over forty. Ristolainen was known to spend more hours training than the top skiers, just over a thousand a year. They watched him go. He was giving it all he'd got, diagonal striding even though he was on the flat, with long, jerky steps; a real slogger on the track. A few seconds later he was out of sight, behind the wall of dull, gray light and densely falling snow. It could barely be called daylight.

Ristolainen's indifference to the weather impelled Elsa to make a half-hearted attempt. She went two hundred meters, stopped, turned back, and said it hurt her face too much and that the track was too slippery.

It was simply an entreaty on her part, a request to be let off, just this once, which was why she had still not divested herself of her skis and poles. Then Ragnar bellowed at her in a way he seldom did: "If it's good enough for Jyrki Ristolainen, it's good enough for you!"

His eyes were ablaze as he bent down, roughly pulled off her skis and strapped them to the top of the car. On the way back he gave her no relief, no alleviation, but sat in stony silence.

As soon as they got home, Elsa took her skis with her to the field below Paradise, where the blades of grass were sticking up through the powdery snow. Here, the track was not skid-prone, there was no track at all, and the wind was almost as fierce as on the golf course. She slithered round for a pointless half hour. As compensation, to show she was voluntarily doing what her father wanted, to show her willingness to put in the training.

When she returned to the house, she could tell that her father considered it a ploy, an attempt to curry favor.

22

Sometimes Ragnar felt he had taken on too great a responsibility: without anyone's permission he had given two new human beings entry to this messy, unpredictable world, where the majority just about made it through, and where life consisted for most of survival and nothing more.

He realized at an early stage that what he needed was a plan. He would be like a benevolent and intelligible state for his children, rationally based and with justice that was absolute: guiding, serving, and determining, all in one. Above all he would induce them not to let life slip past in idleness and pleasure-seeking. They would not be allowed to become like those indolently mutinous teenagers he could see all around him, duped youngsters who thought laxity was desirable just because it was allowed by law.

When Erik and Elsa were old enough to consider their choices for the future, he explained to them that you should not dream of working in a sweet factory just because you liked sweets. They did not understand, and he elaborated.

"The world doesn't exist for you. Work isn't something we do for enjoyment or to make our dreams come true. We work so we won't be a burden on others."

He initially cherished the hope that they would achieve sporting success. He knew how hard it was, how few became winners, how many made the attempt. Sport was primarily a way of escaping temptation and bad company.

The sorriest of all, he thought, were the junkies, hanging about in doped anticipation of nothing. Their lives were over before they had even started, but however hard they tried to turn back, they were lost, because once you had acquired a taste for anything, he knew, it always echoed inside you as a sense of loss. A pit had been hollowed out of their soul, and there the storm would whine and rage forever.

He had no compassion for them, they had made their choice, but he was happy to pay for their pure, state-funded injections and, if necessary, their pure, state-funded drugs, if it meant he could avoid being the object of their infections, thefts, and burglaries.

In the sophisticated strata of society, as always, they nurtured a different view of the situation. In their version, the junkies were a symptom of the malady of the West, their ruination a remarkable protest against the cattle pens of convention, against the very way of life that was Ragnar Johansson's.

That had been their story even back in the late sixties, when he had a newborn baby to provide for and felt a swelling sense of indignation when he read in the paper about Stefan Jarl's documentary and the claim that drug rebels and voluntary deviants constituted a blazing reminder of the slumbering masses, a seismograph in the earthquake of capitalism, a clinical thermometer up the backside of social democracy's sick and feverish society, in which decent working people could not see how their behavior was fattening up their oppressors, duped as they were by the leaders of the labor movement, who ran errands for the capitalists in return for being allowed to run the country as puppets, or think they ran it.

"Just wait," Ragnar had muttered as he read his morning paper. "Just wait until they start losing their teeth and beg on their knees for a flat and a job and three meals a day."

He did not have long to wait. When the second part of the film trilogy came out a decade later under the title *A Decent Life*, all that remained of the erstwhile rebels were ghostly figures sitting in their usual spots with empty eyes, sagging mouths, and twitching muscles. They longed for nothing more than the hateful cattle-pen life of the standard Swede.

Ragnar did not go to see any of the films. The newspaper articles were comprehensive and numerous enough for him to find out all he needed to know. He would have been able to tell Stefan Jarl and his party-hard boys how things would turn out, back in the days when they thought they were creating a better society by scorning duty, exertion, and ordinariness.

His anger grew deep and consuming. Nobody seemed to understand that Ragnar's whole steadiness regime was aimed at avoiding these people's fate. He had never considered himself to have the right to live in a way that left others to pick up the pieces of his failure, to risk anything in the pursuit of a dream that others would have to pay for.

What they did not grasp, the people who talked of those dropout wrecks as rebels, seismographs, and fever thermometers, was that keeping yourself in the zone of the ordinary still came at a price.

It was the result not of privileges but of concerted effort.

The inhabitants of the thinner stratospheric levels did not understand that it was the prospect of a decent life and nothing more that made people labor and stay in line. In contrast with the drug-addicted dregs of humanity and their exalted patrons, most of them were well aware that a decent life was something you had to sort out for yourself.

What the dreamers, the moaners, and the squatters did not understand, those who had risen like a Frankenstein monster from the ambitions of the benign state, was that ordinary people did not put in all that effort to *get* somewhere, but to keep themselves where they were. Duty demanded it.

But now, instead, it was said to be a matter of regret that these young visionaries who had tried to revolt against the bourgeois death machine had been forced to pay such a high price, which only went to show the grinding power of a competitive society, gobbling up everything in its path.

"How the hell can you tell me," Ragnar Johansson would shout at his newspaper and television, "that sitting at Stockholm Central laughing at commuters on their way to work makes you a casualty of society!"

"Are they on about those junkies again?" said Elisabet.

She was more respectful of the writing and speaking classes and less indignant about defective logic, but essentially took the same view as her husband. She could not comprehend why it was worth making a film about junkies in the first place, and things she did not comprehend she left well alone.

"Servants to bow and scrape and clear up after them, that's what they want," said Ragnar.

He folded his newspaper, took his teacup to the dishwasher, cleared away the other china the children had abandoned, and wiped the crumbs and greasy marks off the table. Then he rinsed the dishcloth in the sink, wrung it out, hung it over the tap to air and dry, and started the dishwasher.

He had a particular aversion to crumbs and greasy marks and always wiped them up immediately, exhorting his children not to leave any mess that would dry on.

Wedged between two strata, the nobles and their favorites, Ragnar had been intensely aware all his life of the contempt for the unnoticed, those who were not at the bottom but just above, lacking the destitution and deviance that were the admission ticket to the patronage of the powerful.

The two strata were in manifest collusion, the top coddling the bottom, while both derided Ragnar's middle layer as narrow-minded, hidebound, and an obstacle to those immediately beneath, where no one looked beyond those who were just above. The result was that his layer had to take all the punches from below, as well.

The shameless contempt of the superior stratum for the ordinary, boringly gray people stranded him with a perpetual feeling of impotence. When he found no words to express this, or felt his education inadequate, he could not hit back without confirming his deficiencies, and therefore allowed himself instead to be consumed by latent fury.

At the bottom of the pile, people had it pretty good, it seemed to him. They could do no wrong, and no shadow could fall on them even if they did, whereas his own people, the dull and ordinary sort, had to take responsibility for their own lives *and* for the hopelessness of others.

Ragnar's intense loathing of the judgment that fine folk saw fit to pass on ordinariness was matched only by his loathing of the self-pity of those who blamed others because they did not have anything and were incapable of sorting anything out. Each time he heard those high-flown speeches to the weak, the small, the lame, and the crippled he saw more clearly that it was not the divergent who needed safeguarding and protection, but the ordinary.

It appeared inescapable that the moment anyone reached the higher stratosphere, they were immediately overcome by an immense understanding of every conceivable human shortcoming, except that of being ordinary. And then they reproached him for it.

23

The Stockholmer was the plebeian of cross-country skiing, the Norrlander the aristocrat. At the age of twelve, Elsa had still to compete against anyone from Norrland. The first time was in Sundsvall, at a major event in which all the best skiers in southern and central Sweden were competing. Ragnar had entered her because it was high time she faced the moment of truth. She needed to compare herself with the best in the land.

His daughter was sick with nerves ahead of the start and had barely been able to get her porridge down that morning, but Ragnar thought things would go well, because sport was not based on arbitrary judgments; everything lay in your own hands. On the evidence of her previous achievements, he judged Elsa's capacity to be at the maximum level it could be for a girl of her age, so if anyone was better it could only be marginal, however much of a Norrlander they were. It was their nobility that was causing her anxiety, he suspected, the idea of their supremacy. In her head they already had an advantage, simply by coming from Ångermanland, Jämtland, Västerbotten, and Medelpad.

He was familiar with the sensation, having often experienced the same thing, and he recognized himself in Elsa.

But this was sport. Here, nothing was decided by lineage, or who you knew, only by how well you trained. A number of the participants had parents who had competed in the national team in the 1960s, something the local press was always keen to emphasize every time the young skiers' names came up. "A real chip off the old block," they said, and "great things await this youngster of the noblest stock," and "a true skiing thoroughbred."

It was ten o'clock, the morning air was a grainy gray, and the temperature minus two, but it had thawed in recent days, so waxing was difficult; there was a sprinkling of new snow like granulated sugar that would make it extra heavy going on the body-bending course, with all those steep uphills where the snow gave way under your skis. The icy snow after the thaw called for a thin layer of klister under the hard wax, but not so much that it would catch.

Ragnar and Elsa had arrived in very good time to try out skis and choose the pair with the best glide. Elsa had warmed up and memorized the course. Ragnar could see she was as tense as a taut wire. Ten minutes before the start, he planted himself in front of his daughter, put his hands on her shoulders, looked her in the eyes and said: "Elsa. You mustn't be scared. They're not superhuman just because they come from Norrland. They get tired, too. They get more tired than you. No one can pull away from you."

She nodded, and he made his way onto the course, where he would be giving time checks.

And he was right. They got tired, too, more tired than Elsa, and no one pulled away from her, that Saturday in Sundsvall. It made no difference where they came from or that their parents had been Olympic medalists in the relay, and individually, Ragnar Johansson's daughter went faster. Parents could not ski for their children, and inherited titles did not exist here, or did not help, at any rate, and there were no corrupt judges to influence the outcome.

She won the race, and the omen that this and all her other victories seemed to represent provided one of the lasting joys in Ragnar's life, everything that looked as if it could come to pass.

When a family acquaintance, who loved cross-country skiing "because it's so genuine," as he put it, once asked Elsa how good she was, and whether she could count herself among the five best in Stockholm, Ragnar could see his daughter's discomfort at the man's scale being so utterly wrong; if she were satisfied with being among the top five in Stockholm, then skiing would not have been something worth devoting her time to. She had no idea what to say.

He felt her embarrassment inside himself and answered for her, in such a matter-of-fact and measured way that the statement had an air of the indisputable about it rather than sounding boastful: "I'd say Elsa wins eight out of ten races, against any opposition. In the world."

Because his daughter knew her father rarely said anything unconsidered and never ever exaggerated, never said anything he did not believe, and Ragnar knew that she knew this, his words were the heftiest confidence he had bestowed on her. If there was one thing Ragnar believed in, it was Elsa's chances of going all the way.

So powerful, so intense was his belief in them that disappointment risked being bottomless.

Ragnar was good at giving times. As far as possible, he tried to do it for all the youngsters in the club, so as not to favor his own child unduly. He always kept a stopwatch in the pocket of his winter coat. Before a competition he would study the list of starters carefully; for big competitions, he'd do it the night before, and just before the start when it was a smaller competition they drove to the same morning.

If Elsa was starting early in the field, he prepared himself to give the times of those behind her and scrutinized the course map to see where he could intercept her to tell her how she was doing.

If she started after her main competitors, it was easier. Then he wrote a zero after the skier he judged it worthwhile starting to time, and then 0:30, 1, 1:30, 2, 2:30, and so on, according to the starting order. Once the skier allocated the zero passed the mark he had chosen in the forest, he started the stopwatch and wrote down in pencil—ink did not work in the cold—what the time was when those who would arrive at 0:30, 1, 1:30, 2, 2:30 ... 7:30 came by. If the watch showed 0:25 when the girl due at 0:30 passed the mark, she was leading by five seconds, and he wrote −5 next to her name. If the watch showed 0:37 at the mark it was +7, seven behind. That was easy, but if it showed 0:37 when the skier who started a minute after he started the stopwatch, the figure would be −23, twenty-three ahead.

It was crucial to keep everything in order and think quickly, especially if the skier given the number zero happened to have a poor race. Then he had to try to calculate their place in the short skiing time from the mark where he checked the time. Because if the skier who was due at 2:30 passed the mark at 2:05, her lead in the race was not twenty-five seconds if the skier due at 1:30 had clocked 0:55, that is, −35. It meant that the skier who came past at −25 admittedly had a twenty-five second advantage over the one he had started the stopwatch with, but was ten seconds behind the leader of the race.

Giving times was an act of concentration on a major scale; nothing could be allowed to distract, and no one could stand at his side and chat, as some of the less focused and responsible parents sometimes did, to Ragnar's chagrin and surprise.

If there was a matter of seconds between them, Ragnar would shout so loud the whole forest could hear, but above all the skier heard the time. He would stand poised, the stop-watch resting in his hand and his index finger on the button for intermediate times, leaning forward from the waist so he was closer to the track, and bend his knees slightly, ready to run alongside and have time to yell out the times; he would shout them more than once, to be sure the skier would not miss the time check.

"You're leading by three seconds!" he might yell, the sound dislodging great chunks of snow from the spruce trees. "Three ahead of . . . !", and then the name of the skier in second place.

No matter how minor the ski competition, he would devote himself to the task as intently and scrupulously every time. He kept it all on a very businesslike level. He would never shout anything about how tired the competi-tors looked, for example, or that they were on their last legs, or that the skier whose time he was giving would win if she just kept at it. No value judgments, just pure times and sportsmanship. Ragnar took sportsmanship seriously.

One of Elsa's fellow club members, who had an ex-tremely timid father, once said something to her which she immediately passed on to Ragnar: "The good thing about your dad is that you can hear what he says when he gives times. You can't with mine, because he mumbles."

This pleased Ragnar. The volume of his voice in the forest was intended to be heard above the heavy breathing caused by their exertions, above the sound of skis and poles on the snow, and to urge the skiers to squeeze every last drop of energy out of their bodies.

Elsa had once heard a parent say that if there was only a kilometer or so to the finishing line, you could tell a little lie and give the skier the wrong time, so they would put on an extra spurt at the end; if the skier was seven behind, it was better to tell her she was two behind.

When Elsa told Ragnar this, he was very indignant.

"You must never ever lie when you're giving times," he told her. "Never. Not even if you think it might help at that particular moment. The competitors have to be able to rely on the times they are given. If you deviate from that in a single race, then trust is shredded and everything's ruined, and ruined for everyone else, what's more. The skiers need to know that the times they are given are genuine, every time. One lie is enough to sow doubt, and after that there's no point giving any times at all."

24

They were on their way home from the freezing backwoods of Särna. Elsa had won two races in two days, the other in Älvdalen. Harmony reigned in the car. Elsa and Ragnar were accustomed to each other's company. In the colder half of the year, season after season, they would do the rounds of winter sports centers and insignificant little towns for competitions and training camps. They spent hours on the roads to Gimo, Gnarp, Hede, Lillhärdal, Hällefors, Månkarbo, Garphyttan, Västerås, Eskilstuna, Nås, Jädraås, Högbo, Tierp, Storvreta—hours of talking and thinking out loud together.

There was a faint smell of ski wax and bottled gas in the car. They were making their way through the forests of Finnskogarna, heading south towards Mora. Ragnar was vigilant, driving with all his concentration to avoid skidding on the curves. There was dense forest all around them, the trees weighed down with snow, and the fuel warning light was gleaming amber. Elsa wanted them to stop at the first filling station they came to, so as not to risk getting stranded in the cold, but Ragnar was heading straight on to Mora.

There was an OK filling station there, and they would have no trouble making it that far. He only ever filled up at the Co-op-owned OK chain. They had never run out of fuel due to his refusal to buy gas from anywhere but OK, and it wasn't going to happen now, either, but they had often come close. It wasn't for the cash points so much as out of loyalty to the founding ideas of a social democratic society. They generated a special feeling of warmth and meaning in him.

Once they had filled up at the OK gas station in Mora they had their picnic of egg sandwiches and tea from the thermos flask, using the car bonnet as a table. Elsa asked if he had heard that Galina Kulakova was going to retire. She had seen it on the sports news the other evening.

"She won double gold at the Sapporo Olympics in '72."

"I'm sure she's been given a good life thanks to her sport," said Ragnar with grudging admiration. "Maybe a job and a nice flat from the state. In the Eastern Bloc, they reward their athletes, you have to hand it to them."

"Why are they so good, the Soviets? Why are they best?"

Elsa ate her polar bread thoughtfully.

"Because they've got so many to choose from," said Ragnar. It's a vast country."

They drove on, Elsa mulling over why her father's answer was unsatisfactory. On the way through Rättvik it came to her, and she asked: "But the fact that there are so many of them doesn't explain what those who are best do to make themselves best, does it?"

It was of no concern to her how nations sifted out the best, she wanted to know how the best skier had set about becoming the best. There was nothing she could do about the size of her country, but whatever an individual Soviet skier could do, Elsa Johansson from Sweden could do, too.

"No, that's true," said Ragnar. "That's something else, of course."

His perspective on the matter had been that of broad outlines, hers that of individual opportunities. It was not the first time. The same had happened a few months earlier, when Ragnar said there was presumably no change in the election results back when women finally got the vote, because the women voted the same way as their husbands. That was what his mother had done; his wife was also quite compliant, and the girls he had known as a child were all vague and diffuse; they never said or did anything interesting that made him sit up and pay attention.

To Elsa it seemed a strange assertion, but she could not work out what was wrong with it. Then she thought about it when she was on her own before taking up the subject with him again and asking whether the achievement of a particular result was really why people were allowed to vote in elections.

Ragnar found her objection thought-provoking and formulated a counterquestion.

"The reason we vote is to find out what people think, surely?"

It seemed pitiful to him that he, a citizen of the democracy that was Sweden, could not give a proper account of the legitimate reasons for universal and equal suffrage and why it was designed as it was. It suddenly struck him that he did not know whether it was to reach a result that was favorable for the people of that country, or because they should be accorded the right to decide, regardless of the result. Those were two entirely different things, after all.

And why should people have such a right if they could use it to make things worse for themselves?

"So you think women ought not to have the vote because there's no need, seeing as it has no impact on the result?" Elsa asked him after further thought.

"Well, no, I do think women should have the vote. But I don't know why I think that, and it bothers me."

"Why shouldn't they have it?"

"If you get the same result from only men having the vote, then it's unnecessary, isn't it?"

"But there's no way of telling that in advance, is there?"

"No, but it can turn out that way, even if we don't know for sure."

"In that case you might just as well say only women should have the vote?"

By all means, thought Ragnar. Logically: most definitely. But wouldn't there be an awful lot of voting on irrelevant issues, if that were the case?

He really did not know the answer, and it made him deeply uneasy that he did not understand how the world was constituted, or the grounds for human beings' mastering of it.

"Isn't there anybody to ask?" queried Elsa.

"No, there's nobody to ask. There never is."

25

Britain was led by Margaret Thatcher, the United States by Ronald Reagan, and Sweden by Olof Palme when Ragnar Johansson was elected chairman of the cycling club.

He felt honored, he felt burdened, he felt apprehensive, and filled with the opportunity to transform the operation into something rational and modern. The constant rise in fuel prices threatened to be the death of amateur sport, so the clubs would have to do their part to assist. But the other fact of the matter was that some parents never helped out with lifts to competitions; their children always hitched a ride with the families that were more committed, whose cars were already full. It was unreasonable, thought Ragnar, that those who always expected their children to get lifts to competitive events never had to bear any of the cost, while those who provided the lifts had to pay all the expenses.

He sketched out various models and thought through their moral logic and implications. In the end he arrived at a solution, which he laid before the committee at one of the meetings they held on the first Thursday evening of every month. After some discussion, it was voted through. The doubts expressed by some committee members were to do with their sympathy for weakness. Because what Ragnar's proposal came down to was that not being able or willing should come at a price, and that was money that would go to individuals who were strong enough to sustain active lives and had the money to invest in their children's sport.

It was true that there was always a strangeness to the parents who did not drive their children to competitions and never showed up to any club activities; there was something not quite right about them. They smoked and would still be in their dressing gowns late in the morning; their children wore outgrown clothes, the wrong sort of racing socks, badly fitting cycling trousers, and had visible earwax. The mothers were often single parents and had neither cars nor driving licenses.

Doubtless there were understandable reasons for it all, thought Ragnar, but everyone had a responsibility for their own lives, and if you brought children into the world, then you had to take responsibility for them, there was no way around it.

His proposal meant that the slovenly parents could of course lounge at home in their dressing gowns with their Gula Blend cigarettes for comfort instead of taking an active interest in their children, but not at others' expense, nor by letting others render them services free of charge. They had to buy themselves out by purchasing the "lift to the race" service.

One and a half kronor for every ten kilometers was what Ragnar's system required them to pay to the parents who took other people's children in their cars. At two hundred kilometers, the rate went down to one krona. In choosing that cutoff point, he bore in mind that Örebro was two hundred kilometers away, and most of the competitions were within that radius. Ragnar had stuck the point of his compass into Stockholm and found two hundred kilometers to be a suitable boundary.

The payment per kilometer was compulsory; that was its most important aspect: no parent in the cycling club would thereafter be permitted to take others' children in their cars without payment, as a kindly gesture. There was to be no circumvention of the rules and regulations, to avoid any emotional blackmail. If anyone insinuated that a parent was tightfisted for taking money for a journey they were going to make anyway, the person on the receiving end could always cite club rules.

He drew up special forms for the purpose, with columns and rows where you could fill in the competitions you had traveled to and the distance you had covered. The parents could send for these by post or pick them up at the club and then objectively provide the required information, along with account details for the transfer of the payment.

He particularly liked the idea that one could refer to the rules and regulations in their solid durability whenever human caprice tried to muscle in with its transient emotions, pressures, and pettiness.

The system was perfect in many ways. The parents who did not give their children lifts found it more advantageous than driving themselves, because the price was lower than the actual cost, and the parents who were prepared to take other people's children to competitions also found it advantageous, because their cost per kilometer was lower.

After five years, Ragnar stepped down from his position as chairman. Weary, sad, and disappointed. Erik had abruptly given up competitive cycling, despite his success and the promise he showed. It was incomprehensible, a terrible blow. Erik wanted to get out and see the world, he said, not to be tied down but to live his life as freely as other young people did when their school years were behind them. He wanted to have time for other things besides training and competitions, now that he was nineteen.

What he wanted time for was girls, observed Ragnar, for fornication, endless enjoyment, and lack of inhibition.

To crown it all, Erik voted for the Liberals when his very first chance to vote presented itself in the election of 1985. Erik's father had told him that without social democracy, he, Ragnar, could not have afforded to go to vocational school, and they, the Johansson family, would not have been anywhere near as comfortably off as they were. Erik

169

said maybe that was true of the past, but this was a different age. In view of the fact that not only Ragnar but also several of his friends had voted for the Liberal Party in their first election, in the fifties, it was with a hint of provocation but also irritation at seeing mistakes repeated in this unnecessary way that he put into words something he had long held to be true but never before expressed: "We all vote for the Liberal Party once in our lives."

He was relieved, at any rate, that his son had not proved to be homosexual. There had been a time when Erik, who had already reached sexual maturity, had been far too close to one of his friends—in their social interaction they were like a couple of girls, sleeping over at each other's houses and talking the nights away—and Ragnar had remarked sharply to his family, albeit in general terms, that if any son of his were homosexual he would take his own life out of pure shame.

Homosexuality had been permissible by law since 1944, of course, but when Ragnar made his declaration it was only seven years since the National Board of Health and Welfare stopped classifying it as a mental disorder and providing help free of charge to those afflicted.

Ragnar wanted normal, ordinary children and considering all these girls Erik was talking to now, at least that threat seemed to have been averted.

The main reason for his resignation from the club chairmanship, however, was not the fact that Erik had given up racing and opted for idleness and lechery instead. A group of parents in the club had started complaining about Ragnar's set of rules. They called it inflexible and antiquated. In a free, modern country like Sweden, they said, people should be able to do whatever suited them best when it came to lifts and the exchange of money. After all, they said, it was really only a matter for discussion between the person offering the lift and the one accepting it.

Much of the twentieth century now lay behind them, and an era was on its way out. Things were not what they had been. Ragnar Johansson saw that his society, built on diligence and the ability to think, had started to lose its self-belief.

He was no longer at one with his own times.

This "doing whatever suited you best," when there was demonstrably a better way, was an objection for which he had no respect at all.

At the annual general meeting he stepped down with quiet bitterness and was replaced by a younger and more liberal member, who immediately scrapped his predecessor's payment-per-kilometer system and any form of obligation.

26

I t was June, that time both wistful and showy, when Swedish nature had an element of coquetry intertwined with its harshness. The turn towards the dark was not many days away, and it infused Ragnar with melancholy.

The summer holidays had just started, and he was making his morning preparations to go to the airport to pick up Mother Svea's half brothers, who were due to arrive from Minnesota that day. This was a major event in Mother Svea's life. Discovering at such a late stage in her life that she had two siblings in America she had never heard of had shaken her up. A second cousin of hers had been researching the family tree and found out that Svea's father Johannes had lived on in Minnesota until 1969, when he died of old age.

All those years, ever since 1912, her father had been alive in America. Now it was 1983.

She discovered, furthermore, that Johannes Svensson from Rälla on the island of Öland had changed his name to John Swanson soon after his arrival in America; married a Norwegian immigrant, a woman named Signe; and within two years had had two sons, Sigfrid Swanson and John Swanson Jr., born in 1913 and 1915.

Ragnar stood in the arrivals' hall at Arlanda, wondering how to say various things in English. It was noisy and busy all around him, with constant musical pings heralding loudspeaker announcements in artificial voices. He was not used to airports.

And then there they were, the two brothers, one of them tall and fat, the other tall and thin. They shook hands. On the drive into Stockholm, which took just over half an hour, Ragnar tried to converse with them. This proved a trial for him, poor as he was at both English and conversation. He wished Elisabet could have been at his side; she knew the language and was skilled in the art of casual social exchanges. But she was at work, where she used English every day dealing with foreign clients.

It did not occur to him to ask how the journey had been, and if it had done so, he would not have known how to say it in English, and if he had known he would still have hesitated, because he was not curious about how the journey had been. It had presumably been fine, because they had arrived. He managed some meteorological small talk, anyway, saying it was *nice summer weather today*. Then he decided there would be no point asking how the weather had been in America, for what use would that information be?

Mother Svea had told him that one of the brothers, the elder one who was fat and called Sigfrid, could speak Swedish. But Ragnar did not understand a single word the brother said in something that was supposedly Swedish. Still, now they were finally at Tomtebogatan. His shirt was sweat-soaked after the stress of it all, and he had not brought a spare to change into.

The table was set for coffee, groaning under the weight of all the cakes and cookies. Svea had been baking for three days; in addition to the many sorts of cookies and small cakes, both hard and soft, she had made a cream gateau with lots of confectioner's custard and raspberry jam. Custom demanded that it be eaten last, after the smaller items had been dunked and consumed. They drank their coffee from the thin china she only brought out for special occasions, which lived in the handsome glass-fronted cabinet that Gunnar had inherited from his parents.

She had been to the hairdresser's for a shampoo and set, and bought a new summer dress, light blue with a pattern of little yellow and mauve flowers. With an inquisitive and friendly expression in her bright eyes, she observed the men with whom she shared a father. Sigfrid was wearing gray-blue polyester trousers, a short-sleeved shirt, and big rimless glasses with tinted lenses. There was something expansive about him, whereas John was quietly reserved in a way that reminded Svea of her father. He was in a brown suit, the trousers with sewn-in front creases, and a nylon shirt of a nondescript yellowy-beige color. He had been an accountant before he retired, she remembered Elisabet saying when she translated the letters that had arrived from

America in the six years since the half siblings had discovered one another's existence.

They each wrote a letter roughly once a month, Svea in Swedish to Sigfrid, who would then reply in English. John would send a card at Christmas.

The letters mainly comprised news of aches and pains and reports on the weather, never anything personal or anything like the reflections on life and death in which Svea generally engaged, although never when she wrote letters. The letter form itself rendered her solemn and impersonal. Nothing she wrote in her diary on evenings found its way into her letters to her brother in America, because she did not think any sensible person could be interested in what she thought and did. Weather and sickness, on the other hand, were everyone's business.

Svea did not understand a word of Sigfrid's Swedish, either. But the brothers liked her baked goods, and that was the main thing. One of them tucked in hungrily, almost greedily, and she pressed them several times to have more, which they did.

John spoke hardly any Swedish at all, having been born two years later than his brother, two years in which their father sloughed off the skin of his old country.

The very week Svea Johansson found out she had two half brothers in America, she signed up for an English course at the Birkagården Center. Ever since, she had been cramming vocabulary and phrases, but now that the longed-for moment had come, that moment when she was to hear them speak of her father and who he had become in America, she could not produce a word.

She wanted to know everything, particularly whether he had ever talked about Öland and Mother, about Grandmother, Sven, and Svea herself.

Svea had checked in her English book that morning and memorized a few sentences. The brothers did not understand them but nodded sympathetically. It was as if they could not even hear that it was English being spoken, even though she had never missed a single lesson in all those years and had tried to study on her own as well. Should she have put more effort into her homework?

Svea touched Ragnar on the arm and asked him, with a mixture of eagerness and embarrassment, to ask the brothers about her father. He tried to do so, they looked politely perplexed, so he tried again, with more success. He passed on their reply to Svea: "Our father was an honest man and a hard worker."

Svea nodded. She well remembered how hard he used to work, she said. He was always worn out by evening and often had to go to bed hungry.

Ragnar sat there feeling stupid. What they had meant, of course, was that he worked hard, not that he was a hard worker. If only his wife were here, or the children, who had studied English at school. But they were presumably out training at that time of day. He looked at the clock, helped himself to a couple more cookies, and worried that he always ate too much with his coffee, especially when he felt ill at ease.

Mother Svea was thinking about how like her and Sven the brothers from America were. Two years between them, and one of them bony and not keen on sweet or rich things, the other large and heavy, with an enormous appetite for that sort of thing. Sigfrid was the active and vigorous one, while John seemed anxious and passive, just as Sven had always been. Svea felt she had more in common with Sigfrid, and not only because the two of them had corresponded and because he was fat and could speak Swedish or something vaguely resembling it, but also because of a more intangible affinity conveyed by his considerable bodily presence.

When Svea tried at the end of the day to summarize it all for little Elsa, who was not that little any longer and who rang to ask how it had gone, she was not able to recall anything Sigfrid had said, only how he had made her feel. For the first time in seventy years, she had the sensation of being close to Father, whom she had been missing for almost the whole of this twentieth century.

She did not put it into precisely those terms for Elsa. Matters of sentiment or intimacy were not spoken of in the Johansson family, and Elsa was only thirteen and not to be burdened with the concerns of the soon-to-be dead.

Instead, Svea said that it had been fun meeting Sigfrid and John and that the shortbread meringue swirls had turned out nice and chewy, but the rusks had been a bit hard.

"That's what you always say," said Elsa. "But your rusks are meant to be hard. That's what makes them so great. Shop-bought rusks are brittle, yours are hard, and the shop ones aren't as good, if you ask me."

"I'm glad you think that, dear," said Svea absentmindedly, not really attending.

If she had only found out in time that her father had been living and working in Minnesota for all those years, she could have gone over there to visit him.

But perhaps it was just as well things turned out as they did. If God had wanted her to know what had become of her father, He would have let her know while Johannes was still living.

The American brothers were staying at the Amaranth Hotel, by the town hall. They took a taxi from Tomtebogatan; it wasn't far. Svea was relieved when they left, as it had been a day of great tension.

Ragnar stayed on for a while to screw down a hinge that was coming loose. He was so capable, Ragnar, thought Svea, so conscientious and thorough; she was so proud of him, but scared of him, too, scared of the way his eyes would go black and the rage would erupt.

———

They exchanged a few words about the following day, when Svea and her half brothers would be coming out to the Johanssons' house in the suburbs.

When Ragnar had gone, Svea shed some quiet tears. She hoped her half brothers had somehow understood when she told them she had yearned to go to America so badly it hurt. And that the reason their father never received any replies to his letters was that Grandmother hid them as soon as they arrived.

But deep inside she knew she had failed to get this crucial message across. Perhaps it made no difference. The important thing was that she herself understood.

She went to the window and looked out over the bustle in the street. That generally had a soothing effect. It was a warm evening. She liked these dusty summer evenings in town, when everything seemed to have a sharper outline and everyone was on their way to wherever they belonged. There were a lot of people out and about, but at the Co-op laundry down on Norrbackagatan all was silent and dark behind the streaky windows. It would probably close for good before long. People had got so used to washing machines and other modern conveniences at home that they didn't need laundries anymore.

With Gunnar's death, time and existence had ground to a halt for her. This Sweden was no longer hers. Inside she could still hear the clatter of their horses' hooves, the haulage firm's horses, but it was not only the sounds that were different nowadays, it was the scents, the smells, the clothes, the way people thought, acted, and spoke.

Elsa would keep track of which of Svea's words were archaic and not used by anybody else, and which were in public ownership. Svea was the only one who used the word *sowl* for meat and cheese, Elsa told her. The same applied to *tasks, pouring money down the drain, virtue,* and *paragon of virtue.* Whenever Elsa ran errands for her, she would say, "You're a proper paragon of virtue, dear child."

No one else drank their coffee through a sugar lump clenched between their teeth, or answered the phone by giving their number, Elsa informed her grandmother indulgently. "Thirt fifty-nine ninety-seven," said Svea when she answered. All modern people answered with their name. In the Johansson family they gave both their first name and their surname, with clear diction so no one would be left in any doubt as to whom they were speaking to.

Ragnar Johansson.

Elisabet Johansson.

Erik Johansson.

Elsa Johansson.

That was how they answered, whereas Svea answered *thirt fifty-nine ninety-seven.*

"Why do you say *thirt?*" Elsa would sometimes ask her, though it had been a while now.

Well, she was from the past. Rubbish and junk, waiting to be shoveled away. That was how her grandchildren saw her, she could tell, even though they were fond of her. To them this seemed such an obvious way of viewing things that they did not even see a need to hide it.

The new age left no space for Svea Johansson, who had had the misfortune of being young in an era that revered the elderly and growing old in an era that worshipped youth.

They made things pretty decent for old people in Sweden now, of course they did, with pensions and housing allowances and daily health aide visits to change the bandages on your varicose ulcers and do other chores for you. All the same, nobody considered you anything but superfluous.

The evening sun was making one pavement gleam and glisten while the other lay in deep shadow. She felt suddenly dejected at the thought of having to leave this life before long. There was a lot of beauty in it, even though Gunnar had left her there on her own way too early, with all her memories and regret. He had only made it to sixty-eight. Mr. Armark and Mr. Kollberg were both already over seventy-five.

But Mr. and Mrs. Armark read *Svenska Dagbladet*, so perhaps the announcements of their deaths would only be printed there. In that case she could have missed them.

Svea had told Elsa that it was the more refined sort of people who put notices in *Svenska Dagbladet* that they were dead, which had left Elsa looking baffled and wondering what being refined meant. Svea would not have been able to give her a satisfactory answer.

Unbridled as the ragged clouds above her, her thoughts ranged freely as she stood there looking down on life in the street below. She remembered how scared Ragnar had always been as a child that she would fall two stories down to her death when she hung out of those windows to clean the outsides, and how anxiously he would ask if it hurt, being down on her knees to scrub the floor. They ought to invent a machine, he said, so nobody has to do that.

Her daughter-in-law Elisabet had got it into her head that Svea had been liberated by Gunnar's death. Perhaps it came from those notions of women's rights. Elisabet had said that now Svea was set free from all her duties and burdens she could start traveling, take courses, and think of herself.

Elisabet didn't understand, or maybe she was just terribly modern, exactly like Ragnar. Svea didn't want to travel, take courses, and think of herself; she never had wanted to. Duties and burdens were what people had and were supposed to have. That was what living meant.

The reason she had been on several trips with the sewing circle and the church was to cope with the loneliness. Real life wasn't about entertainment and courses, but about living for others, making things nice for them, putting yourself in the service of good.

Svea pulled the window shut so sharply that the glass rattled, and then cleared away the remaining traces of the day's visit.

27

The next day was a Saturday, so Elisabet was able to join them to translate. If the fine weather held, they were going to sit outside in the arbor for coffee. Svea thought it was lovely in Ragnar's outdoor seating area when the sun was shining. That was exactly how she always put it, Elsa had pointed out; it was "lovely in the sun."

She was up early as usual, getting ready with great care: she had a very good wash even though it took a long time now that her body was getting so stiff, put on the other new dress she had bought for the brothers' visit, lime-green with yellow-and-white flowers, clipped on her earrings and pinned on her brooch.

She drank her morning coffee with a feeling of confidence. The dejection of the evening before had given way to expectation. She was going to enjoy this.

Little Elsa came to the door to meet her as she was dropped off by the mobility service taxi, and seemed pleased to see her old grandmother. The pleasure was mutual, though Svea thought there was something odd about the way the girl dressed, not like a girl at all but like her elder brother, and she moved like a boy, too.

It was the never-ending sporting activities that were to blame. They were all mad about sports in this family, just as Ragnar had been, but at least he was a man. They were forever off somewhere on weekends or in the evening and never got a proper rest. The girl arm-wrestled her brother and measured her arm muscles against his, as if muscles were anything she should aspire to.

Elisabet ought to intervene, but there was no point in Svea saying anything. Nobody listened to her, and they would only say she didn't understand the new age, where there were supposed to be no distinctions between women-folk and menfolk. Inside, however, Elsa was gentler, the only one in the family who gave Svea any physical contact and wanted to have proper talks with her.

The meeting with Sigfrid and John went a bit better this time. Svea got various things straight that she had not grasped the day before. Sigfrid had apparently run a company manufacturing ice cream and had won prizes for it, too, if Elisabet was translating correctly, but she was clever so no doubt she was. Svea could not fathom who might be dishing out prizes for ice cream. Was it the people who ate it?

She asked, but no clear answer was forthcoming. The conversation was all rather disjointed, but it didn't matter. Sigfrid explained they had put extra cream in the ice cream and that was the secret.

"Yes, lots of cream makes things taste better," said Svea. "But that isn't a secret."

And cream makes people fat, like it has you and me, she thought.

When they were still young men, both brothers had moved to Saint Paul from the village where Johannes Svensson had settled down on his arrival in America. Then there was something about a twin and a city called Minneapolis.

"No, John and Sigfrid aren't twins," said Svea, which immediately made Elisabet lose patience and exhort Svea to pay more attention. The cities were called twin cities because they were so close to each other. Svea blinked hesitantly and could not help thinking that Elisabet got cross with her almost as often as Ragnar did.

Svea was not entirely clear about what John had done in his life, but she didn't dare trouble anyone by asking. Had he been a farmer? Previously they had heard he was an accountant, but now there seemed to be talk of a farm. Perhaps he did a bit of both. And perhaps it was the cream from the farm that Sigfrid used for his prize-winning ice cream?

Each winter, Sigfrid would drive south in his car to the warmth of Florida, translated Elisabeth. Svea already knew that because he had written about it in his letters every January, before he set off. Florida was good for his gout, he would write. Nobody else was bringing up the topic of gout today, but Svea remarked how awful it was; she had once had it in a toe and it had been horribly painful. Elisabet didn't appear to translate the comment but then Svea recalled Elisabet didn't like talking about illness or aches and pains.

They had a savory tart with a French name that seemed to Svea just like an ordinary cheese-and-ham pie, but it was very tasty anyway. There was green salad to go with the tart, and then they had another kind of tart with their coffee, filled with gooseberries that had been in the freezer since the previous summer.

Svea had noticed previously that Elisabet was very fond of tarts, and that was presumably why they had been served two of them at the same meal, even though it was one too many. You really ought to have something else with your coffee if you'd had a tart for your main course, Svea thought, but that was not how Elisabet saw it. In her view, things could be combined however you liked, and at any juncture she would make whatever she liked best for any component of a meal, regardless of the overall effect.

"Only Sweden has Swedish gooseberries!" said Elisabet as they tucked in.

She said it every time they had gooseberries. It must be a quote from somewhere, but it always sounded as if she were saying it for the first time.

Elisabet translated her exclamation, and the Americans pretended to understand what she meant, but Svea could see they had no idea. Because Svea herself understood so little of what was being said, and the bits she did understand sounded like the sort of thing she heard on TV, she soon

grew tired and disappeared into her own thoughts. She could
see Elsa was looking at the two half brothers with interest
and following the conversation. She wanted to practice her
English, so she had said on the phone the evening before.

And before she knew it, Svea heard the name Ronald
Reagan come up. It was Elsa, asking the Americans what
they thought of the president. Sigfrid answered something
that Svea could not make out, while John, with the deep-set
eyes he had inherited from Johannes, just looked inscruta-
ble. According to Elisabet's translation, the reply was that
they respected the president of the United States, that was
one's duty as an American, and Reagan was a man of common sense.

Ragnar had been sitting there in silence, but now Svea
heard her son make a sound that could only be interpreted
as dismissive. She had always been afraid of that sound; it
was a precursor of a bad mood. Perhaps spurred on by the
sound, Elsa brought Olof Palme into the conversation, and
Svea got the impression Elsa said Palme didn't like Reagan.
But how did Elsa know anything about that?

Svea was seeing the others as if through a misted window. Why did they have to start talking about politics?

Sigrid's face flushed but he maintained his calm, amia-
ble manner. Erik had come into the room and helped himself to an extravagant portion of tart and whipped cream,
and with that cheeky grin bordering on insolence that Svea
sometimes noticed her grandson deploying, he asked their

visitors if they didn't find it odd for the USA to elect a B-list actor as their leader. Or was that normal over there?

"In Sweden, we laugh at it," said Erik in a tone so light, carefree, and dissociated that it sounded condescending.

"Do we?" asked Elsa, who had sat silent and wide-eyed as the subject she had introduced took this confrontational turn.

"I've never heard anyone laughing. I thought we were scared. Of the nuclear weapons."

Elsa really was a lot less worldly-wise than her brother, thought Svea. She had that slightly awkward naivete, but, on the other hand, Svea had no idea where Erik had found his self-assurance.

"In Sweden, actors never become politicians," said Erik.

The atmosphere in the room was tense. Quiet John felt moved to speak. According to Elisabet's translation, he was asking if Erik could be more precise. Was the problem that Reagan was a B-movie actor or that he was an actor? Would it have been more acceptable if the leader of the free world were a more prominent actor?

Erik stroked his chin thoughtfully, and Ragnar said in Swedish that of course Erik meant the strange thing was actors becoming presidents at all, because it was like saying politics was all theater, lies, and false fronts.

"You want me to translate that?"

"No, don't bother," said Svea. "We're not going to quarrel, my brothers and I, now that we've finally met."

Back home at Tomtebo in the evening, Svea sat herself down in the kitchen alcove, got out her battered English coursebooks, and read them from cover to cover, even though she was tired. She understood barely a word of what they said.

It was too late. Everything was too late. She would soon turn eighty.

She decided it was time to get ready for bed, the same routine she had followed ever since her youth, but more slowly now.

The next day, her half brothers would be going with her and Sven out to Drottningholm Palace, and to the open-air museum at Skansen and the city hall. She would be seeing them several more times before they went back to America for good.

28

I n the increasingly well-nourished land where cracks were filled and warped wood was draft-proofed, young people regularly took off on long, aimless trips just for the hell of it. They went Interrailing. This form of travel itself had something far too casual and disorganized about it, which Ragnar found distasteful. But more importantly, he realized at an early stage that his children could not join in this new custom without jeopardizing their sporting activities. Years before they were old enough for independent travel, he started to worry about making them see what was in their own best interests.

One evening after dinner, when he and the children were gathered in the sitting room over homemade rhubarb tart with lightly whipped cream, he began his oration. With that cumbersome solemnity of voice and sentence structure he employed whenever there was something significant to announce, Ragnar told them he had once heard the sports commentator Åke Strömmer on the radio, sharing an important insight.

As a young man, Åke Strömmer had dreamt of seeing the carnival in Rio. There, he would finally get to experience the real world, which did not exist in his own little town of Falun. It took him a long time and a lot of hard work to scrape together the cost of the trip. And off he went to Rio de Janeiro, the city of his dreams.

He saw the beaches and the mountaintops he remembered from all the travelogues. His eyes beheld the sea and the beautiful women in bikinis.

But he soon realized that the sea was dirty and the beaches overpopulated. It was all crowds, petty theft, and cotton candy, shabby stands with cheap goods and dishonest hawkers. The carnival was like the market in Falun, only noisier, bigger, and more crime-ridden. The music was different, it was true, but in other respects it was like every other traveling market he had ever been to.

The carnival in Rio was nothing worth seeing, it was a mirage. He went back to his home province of Dalarna, where he found everything he wanted and needed.

Just as Ragnar reached his final point, the return to Dalarna, Elisabet came across the room, and her practiced fingers began picking the dead leaves off the houseplants. When he had finished, she remarked that your youth was the time to travel, to make the most of it while you could, because later in life you would be stuck.

Ragnar's features tensed, and his face darkened. The intolerable ease with which his wife promoted precisely the sort of thing he was trying to repel.

"That's as stupid as thinking you have to try to kill somebody to see whether it's the sort of thing you want to do or not," he said.

Elisabet, who was bending over a fern on a pine plant stand that Ragnar had made, straightened up and looked at him.

"What has killing got to do with this?"

She looked genuinely puzzled and just stood there, the dead leaves bunched in her hand. Erik, his jaw set, stared down at the floor, while Elsa looked from her father to her mother and back again.

Ragnar wished he could have found some support for what he considered, in fact knew, to be right, but nobody seemed to agree with him. He was straining against the wind. All he wanted was to make his children see that sport did not mean self-denial. It offered more travel than other people would ever experience, and it was travel with a purpose. All that flitting about in search of meaning to plug your inner emptiness led only to yet more emptiness.

He wanted to make them understand this, so they wouldn't have to waste their time making mistakes other people already knew to be mistakes. He could think of nothing more stupid and inefficient than every generation redoing whatever the previous one had done, instead of learning from it.

Seeing other people head straight for their own ruin without being able to help them was for Ragnar like seeing a loose nut and not being allowed to tighten it, or the protruding head of a nail and not being allowed to get out his hammer. It was contrary to nature and just plain wrong.

"Is there any point having a human brain if you're going to behave like an animal, regardless?" Ragnar said.

Elisabeth's baffled expression made him feel foolish, although as far as he could see it was her ideas, the ones she subscribed to as if to a weekly magazine, which were half-baked, not his.

"You have to grab the chance to travel while you're young," she said again. "You've got all your life to be an adult."

Ragnar once again hoped for the support of someone else in the room, but there was none to be had.

"But I would never go to the carnival in Rio," said Elisabet. "Paris, London, or Rome are much more interesting."

Well of course he should have guessed, he thought, that the carnival in Rio was too vulgar for her. It wasn't even good enough to dream of.

Erik looked up with a wry smile on his semi-averted face. Ragnar's son was somehow always half-turned away from him. He was as tall as Ragnar, but youthfulness made him more imposing. Seemingly unmoved and self-sufficient, he shrugged his shoulders in that nonchalant way that provoked his father so much.

"Maybe it was right for Åke Strömmer. But people are all different, aren't they?"

Ragnar shouted out loud: "No! They're not all different! That's the whole point of this story, that no one's different from anyone else. I wouldn't be telling the damn story if it could just be waved aside by saying everyone's different. What a totally meaningless objection."

He shook a menacing fist in his son's face and the wry smile froze.

"Anyone who fancies himself different from all the rest will be sure to pay the price eventually. You have to know that."

Ragnar feared that his son's excessive faith in his own unique character and intelligence would be his downfall. In combination with a winning manner it was downright dangerous, because then there was every risk of not noticing he had not put in enough effort until it was too late.

"If you want to see the carnival in Rio, you should do it," said Erik. "If it's a disappointment, you'll know another time. How else do you find out?"

The father glared at his son's back as it left the room, always on its way somewhere. The boy's mother had also departed, to throw the dead leaves in the kitchen bin. Elsa was the only one left.

"How else do you find out? By what I just told you about. And by thinking."

———

He went out to the shed to tidy up, feeling very much alone as he hung the tools on the correct hooks. The atmosphere in the house had been soured, and it was up to him to put it right. It was nothing he had asked for, having all this power. The family didn't understand how impotent he felt, how all-encompassing his fear in the face of the world where the four of them existed, when all he wanted to do was make sure his children didn't take any wrong steps. He tried to mark out the pitfalls for them, to make them see in time that for ordinary people there was no scope for dragging your feet or starting over.

Elsa knocked on the door and came in while he was busy collecting wood shavings in a garbage bag.

She said it was five minutes until the evening news on TV, and then lingered, running her fingers over the soft bristles of a clean paintbrush.

"I've never wanted to go to Rio de Janeiro," she said.

Ragnar's laugh was gentle. He found Elsa's severity with herself and desire to please him both embarrassing and touching.

"Oh, a lot of people have had fun at carnivals, too," he said. "It's just that no one should believe they can change your life."

She looked at the yellowing posters of matadors, the matadors of his youth that he had brought home from Spain with him. They were all there on the walls of the shed.

"Nothing changes your life. You have the life you have. And that's good enough," he said.

When she had gone, he stood there and pondered.

Elsa took his words too seriously. His admonitions were aimed at the normal degree of negligence, not at someone who never neglected anything. His aim had not been to chastise her into clean living. Those who lived clean lives were always superior, it seemed to him. It was as if the asceticism gave them a kind of nobility.

He didn't want his daughter to be like that. She could well afford to enjoy herself a bit and be less strict. But how could he urge her to do that without contradicting himself?

His advice had never been intended as a collection of laws, but as guidance. He had not reckoned on being so obeyed.

29

Day followed day, season followed season, and thus time passed.

One morning in midcentury, Ragnar was reading *Dagens Nyheter* while he had his regular breakfast of two slices of toast made from home-baked bread, one with marmalade and one with cheese, and two cups of tea. Before that he had been through his morning routine: showered, shaved with his electric shaver, cleaned his teeth, and dressed in subdued, modest clothing that he had bought some years before but that still served him well. Brown gabardine trousers, and a beige, sleeveless pullover with a round neck, made of artificial velvet and worn over an easy-iron checked shirt, all from KappAhl, the company that started in Gothenburg in the 1950s with a slogan that everyone should be able to dress well.

In that day's arts pages, a section he generally gave only a cursory glance to, out of loyalty to his paper, there was an article by a professor. Ragnar started reading it because the headline caught his interest. The content was strange, and he thought he would give up after a few paragraphs, but something held him there, and he read on with mounting wonder. Although the article was far too difficult, it somehow tackled subjects he brooded about all the time, albeit in a different context.

An American professor was quoted as claiming that the moment an adult looked at a newborn and declared the gender of that newborn, then the child's gender was created; it was created in the human consciousness, where all creation took place. The child got its gender by being expressed in language, it said.

"What's this madness?" said Ragnar to himself, experiencing the familiar feeling of alienation in the face of those who expressed themselves publicly about the world.

Elisabet looked up from her reading and asked what the matter was. He gave a wave of the hand and went on reading.

"So if they say the newborn is a dog, does that make the baby a dog, then?"

"What are you reading about?"

Ragnar was thinking, his brow furrowed as if in deep concentration, and he groped for his teacup without taking his eyes off the paper.

"I don't know. It says here that 'material is an illusion' and 'language is the only thing that exists.'"

The article, which was a full page long, also said that humanity only discovered beauty in the eighteenth century. It was called *the discovery of the sublime*. Only then did human beings start painting beautiful landscapes and talking about them as beautiful, and since nothing could be said to be substantiated or even to exist until it had been formulated in language, humanity's discovery of the sublime was dated to the eighteenth century, when the word was demonstrably used for the first time.

He was not familiar with the term *sublime*, but the meaning was fairly obvious from the context.

"It's called *post*-something."

"Postmodernism," said his wife with easy recognition. "They talk about it a lot these days."

She kept herself more up-to-date than he did, and she was always in total agreement with what she read.

"I see it in the paper every day."

"I've never seen it before."

"Because you don't read those sections."

"And now I understand exactly why, because this is the most stupid thing I've seen."

"Perhaps you just haven't understood. People often don't understand what they read."

He lowered the paper and looked at her over the top of his reading glasses. She appeared to have her mind on something other than what she was talking about; she often did that, and therefore failed to hear how it sounded when she spoke. His wife possessed the ability, a boon for her own well-being, of never being disturbed by things she did not understand. Day after day, she swallowed the newspaper whole. For her, understanding things meant talking as if she had, thought Ragnar. It was a kind of magic. Normally the bile would rise in his throat, but this time all he had was a sinking feeling. Was it the same kind of magic as he had just been reading about, where things came into existence by being named? If you said you were enjoying yourself, then you were. If you never spoke of the rotten state of a marriage, then it wasn't rotten.

She was reading about the deregulation of the credit market and Finance Minister Feldt, who had pushed it through. Neither Elisabet nor Ragnar understood what it all amounted to, he was sure of that, yet here she was, saying how competent Feldt seemed. She somehow made it sound perfectly natural for her to be a good judge of the matter.

He went back to the article: "Objects only exist through their designations. They are made what they are by human utterance of these."

"But why do humans utter them, then? Isn't that the question we need to ask?"

All was silence around him.

30

It was Mother Svea's eightieth birthday. She had made the traditional seven sorts of little cakes and cookies, plus cardamom buns, Danish pastries, and a cream gateau. The Johansson family arrived ahead of the other guests. Ragnar gave her a hand with the shower hose, which was leaking, and wound the big wall clock that chimed the hour. Then he dealt with her accounts.

It was May. The trees were coming into leaf, and you could sense it even in the middle of the city.

"I've got enough for my funeral, haven't I?" asked Svea.

Ragnar was her security in a world that was hard to understand. His clear view of life, his sense of order.

"Yes. But we must hope that won't be for a long time yet."

"You never can tell."

She related to death more easily than he did. She wanted to talk about it, whereas he pushed it away.

"Ragnar dear, you're sure I've got enough for the funeral, are you?"

It was five years now since Svea had started feeling too old to go and do the cleaning, ironing, and floor polishing for Mr. and Mrs. Armark in Odengatan and Mr. Kollberg at Hedemoratäppan. She had worked for them for a long time, and it had been a good way of supplementing her income, even though Mr. Kollberg was a terrible old miser. But she couldn't carry on with it forever. In the future, she would have to rely on her pension.

"Yes, completely sure," said Ragnar.

"I'm glad I've got my widow's pension, from your father. I wouldn't have had much to live on otherwise."

"You've got your supplementary pension and widow's pension and old age pension, so that's not bad when you put them all together."

Svea nodded, and wiggled her toes the way she had been taught at the health center, to keep her stiff legs going and discourage the ulcers from gnawing them to bits.

"We have it pretty good nowadays. With all those modern conveniences. Just imagine how people had to toil and starve and freeze in the old days."

"Things were dreadful back then," said Ragnar. "And we're never going back to that."

"Let's hope not. But a lot of it was the war's fault. The First World War was the worst of all wars. I still remember those profiteers crawling all over Öland, making money out of people's misery."

When no one was speaking, the tick of the wall clock made itself heard. It was a delicate old clock, like all the other fine pieces in Svea's home that had come from Gunnar's parents. It was so delicate that of all the people in the world, only Ragnar was allowed to wind it. The clock stopped once a week and then simply had to wait until he next came to visit.

"You've always been so capable, Ragnar."

He did not like it when she said that. There was something cloying about it. A reminder of an irredeemable tie, a possessiveness that dragged him down.

Then the guests arrived, and they all sat down at the table and ate Svea's cakes and cookies, which were heaped with praise, especially the cream gateau. Ragnar found himself in conversation with a youngish woman, who was one of Svea's home health aides. She said that alongside this temporary job, she was studying archaeology at the university. Hearing this, Ragnar asked a question he had wondered about for a long time. It stemmed from curiosity and from aggression towards the studying classes.

"Archaeology," he said.

"Yes, that's right," said the student obligingly.

"So, you people work to abolish your own profession?"

"What?"

"The professional work you all do ensures that you'll eventually be out of a job, doesn't it?"

"I don't understand."

Ragnar cut himself another thin slice of gateau as soon as he had finished his first, large piece.

"Well, you'll eventually dig up everything there is, won't you? One day there'll be no more need for archaeologists."

"How do you mean?"

"They'll have found everything."

The woman looked round helplessly for Svea, mild and kindly Svea who had invited her to this party.

"But that must be the case," insisted Ragnar. "If the archaeologists' task is to dig up ancient artifacts, they'll surely find them all in the end?"

The archaeology student's eyes darted frantically around the room, but the only person listening to their conversation was a girl who looked about fifteen.

"It won't be in my lifetime, if so."

"But what is it you really want to find in the ground?"

"Whatever's there and could be of interest for understanding history, which we all carry inside us and are shaped by."

Ragnar dispatched his slice of cake in a few mouthfuls. He shuddered at the thought of having to handle dirty old used things that had been lying around in the ground for centuries, and what was more, having to spend years studying to be allowed to do so. The archaeologist turned to the person sitting on the other side of her at the table and struck up a conversation.

Svea said that the local Vivo corner shop had closed down. A new shop had opened there, and it was much dearer. Ten öre more for two kilos of ordinary sugar and fifty öre more for fruit. It called itself the Seven Elves, she said. Erik and Elsa laughed and said that wasn't quite right.

It was named after its opening hours: 7-Eleven. Svea looked bewildered, because she knew for a fact that the shop was open from eight to ten.

"I thought it was called Seven Elves."

Renewed laughter from the children. The archaeology student said she liked the sound of that. Ragnar sat and brooded about history not being needed any longer.

"Those long opening hours always make them a bit dearer," said Svea.

31

One Wednesday in October after the last lesson, when Ragnar was sweeping the woodwork room, Erland Borgström called him up to the principal's office. Ragnar finished what he was doing and then took the stairs to the first floor of the school. Erland Borgström sat in his usual battered armchair, sucking on his pipe. Today he was wearing a suit in a large check, brown and beige with a touch of gray, plus dark brown hand-stitched shoes with a fairly substantial sole, to carry the heavier cloth.

"Ragnar Johansson," said Mr. Borgström warmly, gesturing him to take a seat.

When Ragnar heard the click of pipe against teeth, he was suddenly taken back to his own days as a pipe smoker, a time that in retrospect seemed to him carefree and idyllic. He had succeeded in giving up tobacco altogether when the children were little; it would not have been credible otherwise to promise them a thousand kronor each if they reached their eighteenth birthdays without starting to smoke.

"Ragnar Johansson," said Mr. Borgström again. "Woodwork teacher. Man of the People's Home. A worker of refinement in the service of the common good, a carpenter with supplementary qualifications, combining the hands of a practical craftsman with the head of an engineer, working in wood in this country with more trees than people."

Ragnar looked at Erland guardedly. This wasn't how he usually talked.

"Is there anything wrong with that?"

"Quite the reverse, quite the reverse. There are few groups of professionals for whom I have such respect as skilled craftsmen. Myself, I'm all thumbs."

Ragnar waited in silence.

"I want to offer you the post of director of studies here, when it falls vacant shortly. You're the best of them all, Ragnar."

With his clear, innocent eyes, Ragnar regarded Erland Borgström and swallowed. He swallowed several times. Ragnar was fifty-three, and the cold sweat surfaced and overflowed the furrows of his brow.

He replied that the director of studies role, including timetables and shared responsibility for the entire operation of the school, did not lie within his capabilities.

"Oh, it very much does, Ragnar. You would be excellent at the job. Think it over."

On the way home, Ragnar felt anguished. He would never use the word *anguish* for any feelings he or those close to him experienced, but this genuinely was anguish. He had done pretty well in life, the children were not misfits, the hardest part was over. He wanted a nice, quiet time. He did not want to be confronted once again with the moment of truth and choose to shy away from it.

He drove slowly through the town center with no sense of his surroundings, no awareness of the autumn colors, no pleasure in the raw cold that heralded snow and winter, even though snow was what he and Elsa most wanted, snow in the Stockholm region. The ground was covered in slippery leaves, decomposing leaves of bright yellow and brown.

Safely home, he went straight into the shed and worked on the masur birch side tables for the sofa, which he wanted ready by Christmas. He worked on them for two hours.

As they started dinner, thick salt-pork pancakes, he was very quiet. Then he cleared his throat and adopted the formal tone he only used for important communications. He started talking about wood. He explained that wood was a living material. If you wanted a dead material you should opt for plastic; if you chose wood you had to accept the natural properties of the wood.

Elisabet, Erik, and Elsa watched him cautiously and exchanged glances. They were used to his stiff pronouncements, but this one sounded different, desperate somehow.

"I saw an incredibly skillful fake today. The desk in Erland Borgström's office. Even though I studied it for several minutes, it was impossible for me to be sure whether the desktop was wood or plastic. When not even someone who has worked with a material all his life can tell the difference between genuine and fake, then you really do start to wonder."

"There's so much cheating everywhere nowadays, it's enough to drive anyone insane," said Elisabet.

"But if nobody notices it's fake, then it isn't fake, is it?" said Erik.

They finished dinner and cleared away without resolving the question.

When Ragnar had thought for half an hour, he returned to the subject. They were gathered in the living room to watch the important international football match from Prague, a crucial fixture in the World Cup qualifiers.

Ragnar explained why fake and genuine could never be a question of liking or taste, or the transient emotions of the uninitiated. His son had already forgotten his own thoughts and comment from a short time before, but Ragnar had not. He explained that door panels, for example, existed because of the nature of wood, a nature that plastic lacked. Door panels were put in because wood moved, swelling in damp weather and contracting in dry periods, and working in wood was all about understanding and anticipating this. The fact that doors jammed in their frames when the wood expanded had once led to the discovery that door panels gave the wood room to move *within* the door rather than swelling in its frame, since movement was inevitable anyway. The joiner thus had to respect its nature and overcome it.

Plastic doors had no need of panels. They were nothing but decoration and show, a free ride on something devised by humans for its functionality but then mistaken through ignorance for ornament. That was false.

"Plastic doors shouldn't have door panels. It's wrong. A form of lie."

"That's surely for the door's future owner to decide?" said Erik.

Ragnar gave an imperceptible sigh. Erik was all that Ragnar was not; he could get nowhere with him. As a little boy he had been affectionate and interested, but it was many years since he had last paid a visit to the shed, where Ragnar was always working on the cycling gear, waxing skis, or engaged in some carpentry project after school.

Anecdotes from his father's life no longer seemed of any value to Erik, whereas Elsa still had ears for them all, about door panels, imitation wood, bullfighting, and former ice-hockey legends. About the time Rolle Stoltz was caught out by a feint on the centerline and shouted to Lasse Björn, the other back: "Lasse, close ranks!" About Pelé breaking onto the world stage in Stockholm in 1958, at the age of seventeen; about Gre-No-Li and Gunnar Nordahl's ankle injury; about Nacka Skoglund being known as the swinging corncob, the player who could take corners that would bend into the goal, and who took a taxi to cross the street once he was a professional in Italy.

Ragnar braced himself to engage with his son again. Not primarily with patience, but with objectivity.

"Yes," he said tersely. "The uninformed buyer makes his own decision about what he wants. But that doesn't make it right. Not right and not genuine."

"Says who? How can it be wrong if the person getting the door doesn't think it's wrong?"

Ragnar thought with great concentration, trying to follow Hemingway's maxim, *grace under pressure*, and wished he had more to do with his hands. Anger was easier to control when his hands were occupied. A memory came back to him, the memory of a reflection he had made long ago, and he said in a voice that was both dull and final: "It's wrong in the same way as when Jesus says in the Bible that no one puts a patch of new cloth on an old garment, because what you put in . . . how does it go, Elisabet?"

"That which is put in to fill it up taketh from the garment, and the rent is made worse."

"Taketh from the garment, yes."

He had not opened the Bible in forty years, but that story from his confirmation classes had never left him. Things had their own properties and natural combinations, and those were unshakable. Ragnar was interested in all things unshakable, and in distinguishing them from those that it was one's human duty to try to shake.

"But we don't believe in the Bible, do we?" exclaimed Elsa, with her unfailing ability to be constantly taken by surprise.

"It's Grandmother who believes in that."

Ragnar again gave full consideration to the remark. Then he said: "It's not being in the Bible that makes it true, but being true that means it's in the Bible. That's a fundamental difference, Elsa."

"Gah," said Erik. "Isn't that just a load of old crap we've left behind us now?"

The next day, Ragnar cycled to work fifteen minutes early, went straight up to the principal's office, and announced that he was not going to accept the offer.

Mr. Borgström looked troubled and said this was an extremely regrettable answer. To Borgström's astonishment, it had also been hurled out with some force, as if by someone who had taken offense.

Just because other people believed in you, it didn't mean they were right, thought Ragnar as he stood there in front of the principal. You shouldn't let yourself be fooled by other people's poor judgment. He felt strangely indignant towards Erland Borgström, and was tired and dejected for several days.

But now everything would be back to normal, that was the important thing. He would have the time and energy to help his children with their chosen activities.

There had been a time when Ragnar felt closer to his son. Erik was nine when Ragnar told him Ernest Hemingway had shot himself by putting a small-bore rifle in his mouth, and that Ragnar's own grandfather, Gunnar's father, had done the same thing when the haulage firm ran into difficulties in the 1910s. He had left his family devastated and destitute.

He told his son that no human being had the right to take their own life, because people were bound up with each other, and every single person therefore had obligations to others. They were not free to do as they wanted.

Erik listened earnestly and asked only one question: whether Hemingway had had unusually long arms that made him able to reach the trigger with the rifle barrel in his mouth.

No more was said on the subject and they never spoke of it again.

Even Ernest Hemingway ran away and chose the easy way out, thought Ragnar. Even he failed to maintain self-discipline to the very end. Or was it the reverse? Was it the moment of truth he had dared to face by shooting himself?

Ragnar was suddenly unsure how to see it.

32

The two masur birch side tables for the sofa were ready in time for Christmas, completed in secret in the cramped shed, where they were kept out of sight under tarpaulins. Their legs were slender, tapered at the base but strong nonetheless, their design was elegant and advanced, not striving for effect; below the tabletop there was a shelf made of flat strips of wood, for newspapers and magazines.

Ragnar was satisfied. No one could think them anything other than beautiful.

Which made it all the more crushing on the evening of Christmas Eve, just before the traditional rice pudding, when his wife proved less than happy with the tables, which had just been unveiled with a great sense of expectation.

It was the end of September when Elisabeth let slip in a subordinate clause that some new side tables for the sofa would make the place look nice. Without saying anything, Ragnar ordered the materials the very next day.

Whenever Elisabet was disappointed, her body moved jerkily and her voice grew shrill. The tables were too high, she thought, and too light in color, but she made an effort to praise his skill even so, although in such general terms as to be insulting, because the implication was that he had failed this time.

Christmas Eve was ruined, and the rice pudding was left to go cold while Elisabet ran the palm of her hand across the tabletop with its exquisite grain, pressing so hard that her wedding ring threatened to scratch it, even though masur birch was the hardest of all woods and the surface had a protective finish, too. It was as if she were trying to lower the height of the table with her bare hands.

Now she was insisting how lovely the tables were, but it was too late, and she misjudged the modulation of her voice. She had never had complaints about any of his crafts-manship before, and always held it in very high regard, but she had clearly expected the tables to look different, she couldn't explain how, but these were not like the ones she had seen in the Svenskt Tenn shop in August.

Christmas Eve the previous year had turned equally sour. On that occasion, Elisabet had bought Ragnar an expensive wristwatch, because his other one had stopped working. In keeping with her habit and ambition, she had gone to the more upmarket stores and come away with a watch that was far too grand. It had cost six hundred kronor, and he sat there heavy-hearted, slumped deep into the sofa, staring at the object, nestled there in its case. He didn't want an expensive watch. He didn't want anyone to think he was using a watch to attempt to be somebody he was not.

His despondency had settled like a cloud of poison gas over the house.

"Well change the watch, then," Elisabet had snapped, hurt and wronged and reminded of all the things forced to take a back seat in her life: floating in a higher sphere, not being oppressed by the small-mindedness of the village.

"Change it, for God's sake, and get the watch you want!"

She had bought it with the money she regularly saved from her salary in a separate account, for when she felt like treating herself, so that not everything she earned went to food and other household items.

"How could you even think I'd want to go around with a watch that cost six hundred kronor when you can get them for a hundred?"

"Change it!"

He went and exchanged it for a cheap and basic digital watch made of plastic, and returned the rest of the money to her.

But that was the previous Christmas. This was a new one, and the two tables were placed at either end of the sofa.

33

On the Friday evening Olof Palme was shot dead in Stockholm, Ragnar, Elsa, and Elisabet were up in Umeå for one of the most important competitive events of the year.

Ragnar was asleep when the deed was committed, asleep in his hotel bed. They were spared the youth hostel on this occasion because the club paid for accommodation for the more major competitions.

He did not sleep peacefully because Elsa was about to compete, but neither was he particularly uneasy, either about how she would get on in the competition or about the social democratic People's Home, which seemed solid.

Early the next morning they heard that the prime minister was dead. Ragnar felt a deep sense of shock, as if he were being turned inside out. He therefore threw all his mental energy into mastering it, so nothing would divide his attention or disrupt Elsa's final preparations.

As they sat in their hotel room after breakfast, watching the live news reports on television, Ragnar could see that Elsa was shaken. He told her she had to concentrate on the race and on her own concerns. The welding flame must be directed towards the task at hand. She must stay sharp, even though what had happened was appalling.

"Where is it, that street, Tunnelgatan?"

She sounded on edge but seemed very focused; not on the race, however, but on the incident in Stockholm.

"Opposite the post office," replied Elisabet, as if Elsa would know where the post office on Sveavägen was, but Elisabet often displayed this inability to see things through others' eyes and know what information was relevant for them. Her lack of pedagogical awareness was all but incomprehensible to Ragnar.

"It's a hundred meters north of where Sveavägen crosses Kungsgatan," he said.

"Come to think of it, I don't know where Sveavägen is, either," said Elsa.

"But Elsa. You're a Stockholmer. You must know where Sveavägen is."

"If we'd been at home, we could have gone in the car to see where he was shot."

"But we're not at home; we're in Umeå for one of the biggest competitions of the season. So now let's stop thinking about this."

"Maybe they'll cancel it," said Elsa, and Ragnar could hear the hopefulness in her voice.

"Of course they won't. Not when people have traveled from all over Sweden. It's out of the question."

They drove the short distance to the arena. For anyone who had not heard the news, there was nothing particularly noticeable at the ski track, with its deeply forested parts and high banks of snow. But the initiated could sense an unusual silence around the finishing line, uncertainty in the air. At a meeting that morning, the judges had decided to run the race as planned. They defended their decision by citing Olof Palme's love of sport, including competitive events, and his faith in young people.

"He would have wanted us to go ahead with our races today as planned," the judges told each other and anyone who asked.

Ten minutes before the start, a voice over the loudspeaker announced a minute's silence for the fallen prime minister.

Ragnar put down what he was doing and straightened up. The gravity of the moment impressed itself on him profoundly. He all but stood to attention.

Admittedly he was distinctly out of line with Palme's views on the Third World. They stemmed from an elitism that was not his. The Third World could surely introduce its own rational form of order that would do away with superstition and the poverty it caused, just as Sweden had once done. It was beyond Ragnar why the leader of the Social Democrats felt this strange sympathy for the follies of faraway lands when he was so vehemently against such things on home territory, but he realized it was somehow linked to that primitive summer cottage on Fårö island.

And none of this mattered in the least anymore. To his surprise, he felt the sting of tears in his eyes.

He thought he could see Elsa in the distance. She was warming up. He saw with dismay that she was not standing still, but carrying on with her warm-up as if the minute's silence did not apply to her.

All the youngsters in the racing area were in the same brightly colored outerwear, so he could not be entirely sure. He would never mistake her skiing style for anyone else's, but she was some distance away and it was possible he was wrong.

He hoped so.

The next day they went home, driving all the way from Umeå. There was talk on the radio of the hunt for the murderer. The previous evening had been grim, and the atmosphere in the car was strained. They had covered a hundred kilometers, a hundred kilometers in which Ragnar had stayed silent, in the way he only did when he was working on his anger and testing its fairness before he let it break loose. They were about level with Örnsköldsvik when he began to speak, in that tone he employed for particularly serious matters.

"I deplore the young people of Sweden. I really do."

He turned down the radio, on which the lead investigator was holding a press conference.

"I deplore the young people of Sweden, who can't show respect even for a murdered prime minister."

For a good while, no one in the car said anything.

"I really hope that you, Elsa, were not one of those still skiing around as if nothing had happened."

He paused briefly.

"A minute's silence doesn't just mean not speaking, it means standing still and stopping all activity. One minute, everyone can manage that."

Another pause.

"A minute's silence also means not thinking of yourself for that minute, but of the person who's died. That's what a minute's silence is."

He looked straight ahead and kept both hands on the steering wheel. The hills of the High Coast rose to meet them, one by one.

"It was nothing less than a scandal, what we witnessed yesterday. With everyone still skiing round as if it was a matter of complete indifference that the leader of the country had been murdered."

Not once while he was speaking did he cast a glance at Elsa in the back seat or Elisabet in the seat beside him.

"Unbelievable self-absorption."

Elisabeth had nothing to say, nor Elsa. All the way to Gävle, the air in the car was hard to breathe. That was where Ragnar remembered that he had exhorted Elsa to think only of herself and her welding torch, and not let herself be distracted.

He had not been consistent, he realized, and after that the tension in the car eased a little.

E lsa's race result had been acceptable. Second place, in competition with the best skiers in the country, two seconds behind the winner over a fifteen-minute race. The expectation had been a win, but she was there in the top placings. Sixteen years old and in the top placings, thought Ragnar. It was no guarantee of anything, but if you weren't there at that age you could be sure you wouldn't reach world elite level.

In actual fact, he thought, she really needed to be further ahead of the other skiers from Sweden if she was going to get anywhere in competition with Soviets, Finns, and Norwegians. It wasn't good enough to be fighting over differences of seconds with domestic rivals.

So Ragnar was wondering about a new training regime for next year, more sessions but shorter, higher intensity, more interval training. But above all she needed to shed a few percent of her subcutaneous fat. That would gain her up to a minute over five kilometers on a hilly course. The senior elite were thinner than Elsa, their bodies harder. He had noted that when he recently saw them in the flesh at a competition in Borlänge.

He wished he could lose the weight for her and deplored the fact that every individual had to deal with their hunger themselves.

The hardest thing for Ragnar was that someone else had control of his happiness. He knew Elsa thought he was the one who made decisions about her. But in reality, she was the one directing him. By having power over the one thing that gave him lasting pleasure in life, his daughter owned him without knowing it.

34

The next day, the Johansson family watched all the news bulletins and bought all the evening papers, which they did not otherwise do.

One fact many of them emphasized was that the way the prime minister was shot, in the back, was the most cowardly of all modes of operation. Elisabet, too, repeated this several times: that it was the height of cowardice.

Just like her father, Elsa would cogitate before formulating a question, and when it came it was, as with Ragnar, not rhetorical but on the contrary so fundamental that it was often dismissed as rhetorical, or even assumed to be ironic and full of intentions and subtexts, although that was not the case.

Elsa asked what made it worse to be murdered in a cowardly way rather than a brave one, and for whom it was worse. Ragnar, familiar with the uncomfortable situations she generated with her questions, always took the trouble to try to understand what she meant, and to answer them. This question was a hard one, and he groped for an answer.

"There's a code of honor. For every situation. Even when someone's committing a bad act, they can do it in a way that's more honorable, or less. That's what people mean when they call it cowardly."

"You mean would it have been better if Palme had been shot from the front?"

"No, but more honorable. If you're going to shoot someone, you should at least look him in the eyes."

"Would we have thought it was less terrible if it had been done more honorably?"

"Probably not."

"For the person being shot it doesn't make any difference which direction the shot comes from, though, does it?"

Ragnar agreed with her on that.

"So it's for the rest of us it makes a difference. If we're going to put up with murderers, they must at least be honorable?"

He assented again, increasingly unsure of what they were talking about.

"Well, I don't think I understand what we gain by murderers sticking to the code of honor for murderers."

Ragnar admitted that it was hard to understand the real meaning of that.

"Oh, it's just something people say," said Elisabet, who had been half listening, half engaged in her own thoughts, and did not consider the subject worthy of time and brainpower.

Elsa was silent. Ragnar, too, was pondering the nature of cowardice and the concept of a brave murder. A minute or two passed, and then Elsa said: "It sounds as if they all think it would have been better for him to be shot from in front, because everyone thinks it's better to be brave than a coward."

"Yes, that's certainly what it sounds like."

"But it must depend what you're trying to achieve as a murderer, surely? The person who fired the gun presumably chose his method to be certain of killing Palme?"

Her insistence was wearing, even for Ragnar, who was generally interested in that kind of question. There was a risk of Elsa turning out a bit outlandish and different in her tendency to plow on in that knotty way of hers, which rarely went down well with those around her.

"If you wanted to kill someone, you ought to opt for the most efficient method, oughtn't you?" she persisted. "If the murderer had shot him from the front, at close range, it would presumably have been to let the victim see who he was. But why should he do that? This murderer maybe just wanted to be sure he would succeed. Does that make it cowardly?"

"People say it to console themselves," said Elisabet. "To help them cope with the ghastliness of it."

"People say an awful lot of things without knowing why," said Ragnar. "You'd better start getting used to it."

"But people surely mean *something* by what they say?"

"They mean something," said Ragnar, "but not what they actually say."

"All they mean is that it's detestable," said Elisabet. "They want to sort of spit it out. You needn't be so literal all the time. You and Ragnar are too literal. Sometimes it's better to try to catch the spirit of what's being said, not just the words that are spoken."

Ragnar glared at his wife and gritted his teeth.

An innocent man remained locked up in Kronoberg jail as statesmen from all over the world arrived in Stockholm. The funeral was going to be broadcast on television, two weeks after the murder. Elsa really wanted to watch it, but she was registered to compete at an event in Västmanland, and it was simply not done to miss competitions for which you were registered.

Besides, Ragnar was sure she could not be more interested in a prime minister's funeral than in a skiing competition, so the matter was not discussed. Ragnar, too, would have preferred to stay at home on this occasion. Here they were at something no less than the heart of contemporary history. But he did not intend to let his own trifling wishes get in the way of Elsa's higher goal. One should not give in to fleeting fancies; it never ended well.

And thus, for each other's sakes and for a greater purpose, father and daughter set off for Västmanland at 7 a.m., that Saturday in mid-March.

That evening when they were back home, eating macaroni with crisp-fried bacon and ratatouille, Elisabeth told them about the cortege, the coffin, and the new prime minister's speech and set jaw.

Ragnar's daughter felt as if she had a kind of void inside her, where something was missing. She envied her mother, who had been able to stay at home and let herself be pervaded by what was going on in the world, without needing to perform, without having to push herself to exhaustion on yet another Saturday. How nice that sounded, how pleasant.

On Sunday they were off to another event, in the north of Uppland. Elsa's competition outfit was hanging up to dry, and the minute it was ready she would put the garments in the right order on a chair so there was nothing to delay them the next morning. She repacked her bag with a change of clothes for afterwards and went to bed early as usual, in order to be fully rested.

Both the weekend's races were insignificant in character, with easy victories. But you had to compete all the time, as much as you could and regardless of the status of the event, Ragnar believed. It was vital to maintain continuity so as not to let yourself down. Competing could not become a big deal, which was why you had to do it frequently. It was also a matter of respect for your sport: you had to take part in the competitions that were offered and not reject them as too small.

It was only in competitions that you faced the moment of truth, he said. That was when you could force yourself towards the most extreme limit and find out where it was, so you never started deceiving yourself, lulling yourself into a false belief in your own capacity. That capacity had to be constantly tested, even if it was sometimes a test of no great value.

35

I reckon it was the police," said Mother Svea when the murder hunt had been in progress for four weeks.

It was a Sunday in late March, and the Johansson family had come round for an early dinner. An orb of fiery orange had reappeared in the sky after an absence stretching back to October. It was equally unexpected every year, and its warmth just as delightful.

Svea served pork fillet in its own roasting juices with fried sweet onions, boiled potatoes, and tender green peas, followed by vanilla ice cream with homemade fruit compote.

"I reckon it was the police who did him in," she repeated when nobody reacted.

"Why?" asked Ragnar.

"They didn't like Palme. I've read about it."

The fact that Mother Svea thought it was the police made Ragnar think it wasn't.

"You think the police would murder Palme just because they didn't like him?"

"Wouldn't they have made a more professional job of it, if so?" said Erik. "The police surely wouldn't need to kill him that way, like in an old backstreet brawl?"

"Maybe they wanted it to look like a backstreet brawl," said Svea.

Ragnar looked at her sharply, taken aback.

"Oh, come off it," he said. "This isn't Latin America or the Middle East."

"I still think it was the police."

She said it in the resigned yet defiant tone of someone who is never listened to but still knows her own mind. Ragnar did not think anything, but was relying on the facts that would soon come to light in good order, as befitted a respectable country.

His agony directed itself elsewhere. Elsa was eating too much, eating as if this were her last meal, and taking so much ice cream that there wasn't enough for other people. He had recently told her that she would have to lose several kilos before the next season to attain the body-fat percentage of an elite sportswoman. And now, despite that, this indiscipline he did not recognize. If only he understood why.

A month before, he had read the weight of Sweden's leading female skier at the senior level in an article and asked Elsa what she weighed; it turned out to be as much as five kilos more, even though they were the same height and the senior skier had in all likelihood developed more muscle over time.

Seized with desperation at not having the power to do anything about it himself, he had told her exactly what he thought: "This won't do."

After that, Elsa had eaten nothing but defrosted diced root vegetables with clear broth for several days, until she finally wolfed down a pizza and rammed the box into the bottom of the trash can under some newspaper, where Ragnar found it the next morning.

He saw that he would evidently need to tread carefully to make sure she didn't end up with those strange problems the newspapers wrote so much about: young girls who were trying to lose weight but binged on unimaginable amounts of food instead and then made themselves throw up before the energy turned into body fat.

But still she somehow had to get rid of those kilos, or all her training would be in vain.

"The police have those machines," said Mother Svea, "that they talk into. On the street."

Ragnar said that was enough and informed her somewhat brusquely that in Sweden the police protected the prime minister; they did not murder him.

36

I t was only after a considerable passing of time that the little shifts became evident, the ones that go unnoticed as they are happening. The hair thinning, the stomach growing a little paunchier every year. In the same way, the whole of society was slipping out of Ragnar's hands, but so gently that the process was barely detectable.

The party officially known as the Social Democratic Workers' Party won the election one final time in the old era by dint of a huge reforming push. The party's achievement was living on borrowed time, and like everything else that is about to die, it kicked and struggled and looked full of life.

Ragnar felt an affinity with the new prime minister from Borås, whose mother had been a seamstress. He even bought a book the man had written about his political thinking and liked what he read; he trusted Ingvar Carlsson.

Erik was now earning his own money and was always on the move, as the fancy took him. Technically he still lived at home, but he was seldom there, except for a change of clothes. In practice, he lived at the homes of various friends and girlfriends.

Elsa had just turned eighteen and come of age. That meant two things. It was time to prepare for her driving test and to join the queue at the Stockholm City Council Housing Agency. Ragnar taught his children to drive himself—no expensive driving lessons for them—and it went well on each occasion. In their second lesson, he directed Elsa that her lane changing had to be more distinct; she couldn't dither between lanes; a few months later, she had her driving license.

It was only sophisticated types who thought they didn't need to take their driving test at eighteen, those ethereal beings in the higher stratosphere with their admirably eco-friendly habits who always found someone else to drive them.

The Housing Agency posed a more difficult problem. He dreaded the day Elsa would leave home, and his old life would vaporize into a mere memory.

Yet he was the one who went and put her name down on the accommodation waiting list after her eighteenth birthday. The reason for this was that she had not done it herself, although he had urged her several times and felt mounting astonishment as she failed to get around to it. The pains he had taken to make his children grasp the realities of life had clearly not helped, because Elsa seemed to find it hard to accept that apartments did not simply fall from the sky. The weeks went by, and day after day he would come home from work to find Elsa lying on her bed, reading, before going out to train, listless and out of form.

She did not go into town to the Housing Agency.

They had an argument about it, in which Elsa, who had always met his eyes with that innocent, wide-eyed gaze, looked away and mumbled that it really ought to be possible to get somewhere to live without having to wait in a queue. To this she appended the usual litany about "this country" and its never-ending queue systems, which Ragnar took as a personal accusation and affront. He felt a particular sense of shared responsibility for the way Sweden worked, having voted for the current order of things for decades and supported its spirit wholeheartedly. And nothing annoyed him more than lazy comments of that kind about everything that was wrong with his country.

They resulted, he told his daughter, from a foul-smelling brew of vanity and ignorance of the real conditions of life and the difficult, well-weighed choices that had been made to ensure things were as good as possible, even for people like insignificant little Elsa Johansson.

He was in high dudgeon.

"Isn't it everyone's right to have somewhere to live?" said Elsa.

"And who do you expect to give it to you?"

Elsa looked at him with something akin to surprise, but evidently without budging from her belief that she was right and that he was the one not keeping up.

"How should I know?" she said, making it sound as if the question was irrelevant and hidebound.

"You mean the state should present you with some-where to live the instant you need it?"

"Well, we get everything else that's our right from somewhere, don't we?"

This stoked his anger still further, and his despair, but he kept them under control and took himself elsewhere. A memory surfaced of a similar discussion, without rancor on that occasion, that he and Elsa had had when she was little, maybe eight or nine, and the inequalities in Swedes' stan-dards of living were under daily discussion, socially and po-litically. This had led Ragnar's daughter to conclude it was wrong that not everyone in Sweden had the same amount of money, and that the politicians must be at work, remedying this. She had asked her father why everyone couldn't simply have the same amount of money.

"If it's a bad thing that people don't have an equal amount of money," she had said, "why don't they give everybody the same?"

Ragnar had answered her, as always, with precision and in a way that she could apply practically, so that she learned to think instead of having things handed to her on a plate. No one should have things handed to them on a plate.

"Who would they get the money from?"

"They must already be getting money from someone now, though. Different amounts of money. So why can't they all be given the same instead?"

"But if we all get the same, some people will spend some of theirs on Disney comics and others will save it. And then they'll have different amounts again."

Ragnar had often thought he would like to study economics to gain a better understanding, but as with all things theoretical he did not know how to go about it. And the fact that the economists could not agree did not speak well of their subject. They seemed to track political ideas rather than follow the natural order of things. After all, if something was true, it ought to remain true no matter which economist was speaking, but that did not appear to be the case.

The next day, after the last lesson, he took the suburban train to Karlberg and walked the short distance from there to the Housing Agency at the intersection of Sankt Eriksgatan and Fleminggatan. Six weeks had gone by since the first date when it had been possible to apply, six lost weeks that she might one day regret throwing away when the cost was brought home to her.

The task of making the trip into town and completing the procedure was simple and took no more than an hour. Elsa could easily have done it after school if she had not been so wrapped up in herself.

He was back shortly after five and handed her the registration acknowledgment. The estimated wait was four years for a bedsit with a kitchenette in the suburbs, fourteen years for a bedsit with a separate kitchen in the center of town. It was a long time, but either you waited in the queue or you needed other means that he did not possess. What he *could* give his children was the power to act, the capacity to think along several lines at once, and the stamina not to take refuge in the faith and hope that dreams would help against the iron laws of the material world. Nothing helped, except realism and a dogged disposition.

Elsa was embarrassed as she thanked him, and blushed, which made him feel he had not completely failed.

If only he hadn't felt so lonely. It was as if the ground was gradually giving way beneath his feet.

37

Everything of any importance casts long shadows. When Ragnar Johansson's daughter gave up sports it did not happen overnight, even if one individual date marked her definitive departure.

She had now reached the age at which everything had to move to the next step. Instead, everything was going backwards.

School was over and done with, the white graduation cap hung on a hook where it could start to yellow, and she had a part-time job at the reception desk of the swimming pool in Åkeshov. She would spend the rest of her time training hard and laying the foundations for the coming years' concentration on elite-level sport. That was the plan. That was also what she appeared to be doing. She completed her training sessions, though without the passion and focus that had been her hallmark and Ragnar's pride and joy. She was somewhere else, slipping away from him as he watched, and would sit there thinking, her eyes fixed on a point ahead of her, absorbed in some activity that did not look like daydreaming, but something else. It was as if the point ahead of her was actually located in her brain. When she was not sitting like that, she lay on her bed reading, sometimes for hours at a stretch.

That October when, according to the schedule, she should have been in her most intense period, she read Kafka. Wasn't he the very author who deluded young people into thinking misery was the mark of being singled out, and bohemianism an exemption certificate from society's expectations? He thought he had heard something of the kind. The very name *Kafka* had an ominous ring to it. At least Elsa hadn't bought herself that dreadful black T-shirt Erik went about in, with the slogan *Kafka didn't have a lot of fun either.*

Sarcastically, Ragnar asked his son who else besides Kafka didn't have a lot of fun. In reply, Erik merely gave one of his impudent, engaging laughs.

The book Elsa was reading was called *The Trial.* Ragnar suspected it was the kind of book you were supposed to read to be "with it." Elsa's reading felt to him like a pose, because she was not bohemian in her soul; neither slovenly nor brittle, nor with her head in the clouds, but robust and methodical.

It made him dislike her incessant reading even more. Elsa was as bad as he was at being someone she was not, and he despised the fact that she was now pretending an interest in books and films. This was the hardest part to bear, because he did not want to despise his daughter.

Late one afternoon, when the rain was spattering the windows and the autumn gales were tugging at the old cherry tree outside, he went into Elsa's room. She was lying on top of the tidily made bed, reading the end of *The Trial*.

"You read such difficult books."

"It's not as difficult as people think."

"Have you been out training today?"

Ragnar knew she had not.

"Not yet. I'll go out soon."

"You fancy finishing your book first?"

She ignored the tartness of his tone.

"I won't have time to. Every page takes quite a while to read. It's a high-density text, this one."

Density, thought Ragnar.

"So, what is it you're waiting for?"

He had been noticing the change for some time. Elsa left it until late in the day to go out and train. She did other things. As well as lying on her bed, staring into space, she talked on the phone or caught the bus somewhere. When he asked where she had been, she said she had gone to the library in Vällingby or to the video rental store. In the evening, she and Elisabet would watch the films she had borrowed and they would discuss them afterwards with an absorption that he had never felt for any form of entertainment.

She returned from her dutiful training sessions with dry clothes and not a drop of sweat on her brow. That was not the behavior of an elite sportswoman. And maybe that was logical, thought Ragnar, given that her body was no longer that of an elite sportswoman, but a standard, shapeless, overfed welfare body in which the muscles were no longer visible, but wrapped in a soft layer of surplus blubber.

He hoped for a change, lived in constant hope, but in his more clear-sighted moments he knew it was all over.

One evening he summoned up his courage—it took courage because he was afraid of the answer—and asked what it was that made her put off going out to train until the evening. She replied that she was waiting until she felt like it. Sport had to grow out of inclination and pleasure, she said, because then your training was more effective, not just mechanical.

It was hard for Ragnar to hear her say such things and see her on course for her own undoing, yet not be able to intervene. The same impotent distress as when Erik had stopped competing, three years earlier. It had been awful then, and it would be awful again now.

All these years he had tried to impress on his children that inspiration was not the route to overcoming resistance, only discipline. But they would insist on reinventing the wheel themselves.

He thought and thought about how he could appeal to her understanding of the abilities she possessed, and one day when she came home with three more videos to watch on the next few evenings, he said to her: "You could entertain a whole world, Elsa. Instead, you let yourself be entertained."

She looked as if she was pondering his words, and hope flared within him. Perhaps he had given her the food for thought that she needed. But then she said: "It isn't entertainment, Dad. It's study."

Her gaze was not defiant but sorrowful, sympathetic, and full of a vitality that was lacking in his own.

lsa's sporting activities were now a delay on an action that had already occurred, like a vehicle still propelled forward by kinetic energy even after the engine has been switched off, or a celestial body continuing to shine even after it has cooled and died. But no one had clearly stated that it was over, so Elsa and Ragnar carried out their routines for a while longer. As winter approached, they went to training camps in the north of Dalarna to find the snow and let Elsa get some distance under her skis, as they had done every preseason since she was a child.

It was the first weekend in November, and the All Saints' holiday weekend. Mother Svea had asked Ragnar to take her to the grave in his car, but she had to rely on the mobility service again that year. They were always away for training over All Saints' weekend.

Elsa had pulled herself together and exerted herself more in her training over the past month, both interval training and longer runs; she had come home in a sweat every time. She was still in poor form because of all that body fat, but Ragnar summoned the memory of former heavyweight boxers who had regained their match weight and won back their titles.

Nothing was impossible. Everyone who had reached the top had experienced bad patches and setbacks that they had overcome. He lived on the glimmer of hope that these thoughts gave him.

The problem was Elsa's lack of commitment. There was no sign of real interest on her part. All the way up to Dalarna, she sat beside him in the car, reading a book. The author's name was Gyllensten, which sounded sophisticated. Gyllensten. Not knowing whether Gyllensten was living or dead, who he was or what he had written that could engross his daughter to this degree, Ragnar felt his ill-feeling towards the man growing with every few kilometers they covered. When she occasionally raised her eyes from the book and looked out over the countryside, he felt the schadenfreude of the envious running through him. Not even you can hold on to her, he thought.

They reached the cabin village in pitch darkness. Their cabin was hard to find, and it was a hassle getting the key; it was cold and damp and the bedclothes were chilled through. Everything was inconvenient, freezing cold, and difficult the first evening; that was the way it had always been at these preseason camps, nothing new there. But never before had they had Lars Gyllensten to contend with on top of everything else.

Two training sessions lay ahead the next day. A hazy milkiness showed itself above the mountains for a few short hours, and they had to make the most of them. The training sessions started and ended in darkness. There were no illuminated ski tracks up here.

They didn't talk much.

Elsa ate her breakfasts of porridge with skim milk and reduced-sugar applesauce and then went out to ski her morning circuits. After a low-calorie lunch and a short rest, she started the next session. They had arrived on Wednesday evening and would stay until Sunday lunchtime. Seven training sessions in all.

As soon as she had showered, she would start reading. She had finished Gyllensten and moved on to Henry James. Sometimes she would smile at what she read.

On Saturday she cut short her second session. There was a film starting on TV at half past three that she had not been able to find in any of the video stores, though she had hunted high and low.

When Ragnar saw her, freshly showered and settled in front of the TV with that bright, expectant look she nowadays reserved only for when she was about to watch a film, he reached the end of his tether. He was not spending his free time in the ancient forests of Dalarna to see Elsa watching TV in a cabin that was way beyond his means. He felt the rage burning inside him.

246

"Was the film good?" he asked as they ate a parsimonious dinner designed for rapid weight loss, consisting of brown rice, tomato sauce, and tuna in water.

"Was the film good?" he repeated, feeling the astringent and utterly disgusting tuna against his soft palate.

Elsa replied evasively at first but then gave him a serious answer, as she was seized by a trusting hopefulness that he would want to share her world. She said she would call the film interesting, not good exactly, but interesting. Its director, she told him, had been prevented from doing film work for a long period during the McCarthyite era in the USA. The Communist witch hunt, she added, in case McCarthyism was not fresh in his mind.

Shyly she attempted to catch his eye to see if they could meet in this as they had met in conversations and topics over the years.

"This was the first film he was allowed to make after that, which is what makes it especially interesting. That was the main reason I wanted to see it."

The pretentious use and repetition of the word *interesting* aggravated Ragnar still further.

"It's also terribly interesting," he said, "that you're more committed to watching a film on TV than to your training, even though you're at a training camp."

He saw her wince, but he was past caring about the niceties. The table in the cabin was poorly made and badly screwed together, and barely stood firm as he slammed his fist down on it.

"Are you out of your mind? You think I get in the car and drive seven hundred kilometers so you can watch films and lie there reading?"

Elsa looked down at what little remained of her meager portion. She had eaten quickly, and still felt ravenous, but she was not allowed to eat any more that day.

O n Sunday evening, when they arrived home after a silent car journey, with not a single word spoken, Elsa announced that she was not going to compete or train again for the rest of her life. Then she went into the city center to see a late film, because the atmosphere in the house was unbearable. Ragnar sat there apathetically all evening and went to work like a robot in the days that followed. It was Thursday before he pulled himself together and went out to the storeroom, where he cleaned the old wax and dried dirt from Elsa's skis and then put away the wax kit, wax stand, gas burner, skis, and poles.

As he worked, he listened to the radio as usual. The Wall had fallen in Berlin. People were going through the border-crossing posts and the guards were not shooting them. They were rejoicing, and in the studio in Stockholm, too, there was rejoicing, sometimes interspersed with commentary and analysis. Freedom had triumphed in Europe after decades of captivity, they said.

Ragnar thought, as he stood there, that now there was no hope for the world's poor.

He had always found it easier to identify with the border guard than with the rebel. One followed a carefully devised set of rules and was mechanically scorned, the other broke them and won cheap sympathy. One protected the humble from chaos and disorder, the other pushed off, leaving the more sluggish behind, those who did not become anybody and simply wanted to stay where they were.

If he had not felt so empty inside, he would have wept, but that would have needed a living heart and his felt dead.

Ragnar Johansson no longer had a task; he was surplus to requirements.

39

L ife continued. The years ran their usual course. The Johansson offspring went out into life, searched for a route through it, studied, visited foreign continents, formed bonds of friendship.

Their mother Elisabet Berg Johansson was finally able to take her holidays in places with a cultural history. For two summers in a row, she induced her husband to go touring in the car round the new Europe. They traveled the little back roads of Germany and Holland, visited old churches and ruins, and ate sumptuous German cream cakes and many kinds of spiced sausage.

Elisabet had readied herself with guidebooks and the right sort of shoes. She let herself be pervaded by all the new impressions and would have enjoyed them even more if Ragnar had been in a better mood. But he complained all the time and longed to be somewhere else as he suffered corns and blisters and sweated in the Continental heat.

He found it painful to see deferential cleaning ladies in public toilets and be expected to give them alms, and would ask himself in those same toilets how the German authorities could allow plastic door handles.

Elisabet did not spare a thought for German building standards or cleaning ladies, but continued to be suffused with the delight of expanding her sensory impressions. Ragnar's sullen restlessness was distressing, but she had grown used to it over the years. It made the times when he relaxed after a whiskey in their hotel room all the more precious.

"We're doing all right, you and I," he said one evening when they were staying the night in Berlin on their way home and he was standing at the window looking out over the Kurfürstendamm. "You do think that, don't you? We're doing all right?"

Elisabet, unaware of any problem, offered her warm confirmation, feeling a little embarrassed by this unexpected outburst of pleading vulnerability.

It made his flesh creep, having to play the role of tourist, the ultimate manifestation of emptiness in a meaningless life. Ambling listlessly round unfamiliar places, with no destination in view, looking for reasons for being where one happened to be and finding them in visual impressions of churches, buildings, and monuments. You had time and money but no substance to your life; all that remained was to wander the pedestrianized streets of foreign towns and look at things.

Boredom was his companion once again. All he could think about and look forward to was the next meal, the next stop for coffee and cake. He wanted to get away, but he didn't know where, because there was no direction in his daily life at home, either. He had built up a life and now it was gone.

Sometimes he would see a cathedral and be seized with a sense of amazement how they were able to create something so magnificent so long ago, to construct arches and mosaics in such fantastic patterns, to organize the work and transport the materials to the place without modern techniques and aids, how it was possible for them to have had this comprehensive knowledge of advanced matters, a skill and proficiency in engineering that no one possessed or nurtured any longer.

How had it come to this, thought Ragnar: that all the old knowledge was abandoned in the belief that it had nothing to say or give to people of the new age—just as his own children had done when they rejected him like a prehistoric relic, rubbish to be thrown on the garbage heap.

That was certainly not what he had meant by dismissing the past and embracing the modern. In his youth—surely this was the case?—the new had been synonymous with what was sensible, rational, and ideal. A modern age that lost its grip on the fundamentals was not worth defending.

I t was a great relief for him to get back from those driving holidays. But once home, boredom gripped him still more tightly by the throat, the anonymous shuffle towards death that he had always dreaded but persuaded himself to be the common human lot before doing everything in his power to steer his children away from it.

Erik had been offered a job by a European bank and had moved to Brussels. Elsa still lived under the roof of the family home. Every morning she caught the bus to the university and learned to think complicated thoughts and express them in even more complicated terms.

Ragnar would be turning sixty in six months' time. It was August, and the Swedish election campaign was underway at the same time as the Soviet leader Mikhail Gorbachev had been placed under house arrest by defenders of the regime, who briefly seized control of the collapsing empire.

The People's Party in Sweden had an election slogan: "Free Sweden!" It was in evidence on bridge parapets and lampposts and everywhere election posters were generally to be found.

"Whose bloody freedom are they talking about?" yelled Ragnar one day when he had cycled home from work and seen them lining his whole route.

"Their sign is a total mockery when you look at what's happening in the USSR!"

Ragnar never lacked a target, was never diffuse or vague, because his mind was always engaged in a polemic against something. Elsa knew accordingly that she was the intended recipient of the statement "Whose bloody freedom are they talking about?!"

She was studying linguistics and the history of ideas, and independently reading books on political philosophy and the founding of the United States.

"The individual's," she suggested.

"So, what freedom do you as an individual lack in Sweden, then? The freedom to change schools whenever you feel like it? To be provided with a competing postbox to post your letters in? To go to a different doctor from the one you've been referred to, until you eventually find one corrupt enough to put you on sick leave for a grazed knee? Eh?!"

More and more often, people would leave the room when Ragnar was talking, and lately even Elsa had been running out of steam. She retreated into her room, and Ragnar, left sitting in front of the television, watched her go. Elisabet tended her houseplants.

He was still in unutterable pain over his children's decisions to change course and give up sport, and there was no succor to be had. He was a broken man, a man who on one unfortunate recent occasion had roared at Elsa that he had aged ten years in the space of one, and pointed meaningfully at his hair and face.

The incremental growth of unfamiliar words and sophisticated ideas continued with every book Elsa read, and his fury pooled and glowed inside him like lava. She reminded him of a little girl dressed up in her mother's bra and high heels, tottering about without realizing how she came across to other people.

The eruption came one evening over dinner, when Elsa used the word *dogmatic* and straight afterwards the word *emotive*. Elisabet, who liked unfamiliar words and any opportunity of learning new ones, was taking an active part in the conversation. It was clear from the context that Elsa was talking about narrow-mindedness in one case and feelings in the other. Those had words for them in Swedish and it ought to be perfectly possible to use ordinary words for ordinarily occurring things. He felt as if fire was spurting from his eyes and lava flowing from his pores as he got to his feet at his side of the table: "But do you know what an *emulsion* is?! Do you?"

He had often worked with emulsions but had never looked up the word; it was as if the dictionary did not exist for him. He mistrusted reference works in the same way he mistrusted disconnected facts about the world. Science changed its truths all the time and was not entirely to be trusted, while logic and rationality always stood firm. The ultimate truth of the world was as it was, regardless of what the research was saying at the time. It had to be thought into existence and manifested through inescapable connections, not plucked from individual items of measurable data colored by feelings, wishes, politics, ideology, and prejudices.

Elsa did not know what emulsion meant and seemed frightened by this anger that had sprung from nowhere. Ragnar could see that she thought he was being unfair, absurd. Deep inside he thought she was right about that.

What he had been trying to say was far too complicated to explain, and too shameful; in actual fact it was just this one simple thing, namely that what he said had a value, too, even if it was not what anyone studied at university. His wish was not to shout and carry on, but to stop her from joining the classes of the remarkable and starting to look down on people like him.

In his own sphere, Ragnar was never careless about ensuring a term was exact. Nothing but the right term would do for a rasp, a file, or a pair of pliers, for a tack or a nail or a sheet of chipboard. He would never have stooped to using approximate terms for material objects.

But these words were not a mockery of the ordinary. They were something completely different from the terms in the abstract field of the remarkable.

The following day he went and bought a paperback edition of Jean-Paul Sartre's *The Wall* as a Christmas present for Elsa. He had heard her telling Elisabet that she wanted to read it once she had finished *The Words*. Ragnar wrote the name and title on a slip of paper and cycled off to Persson's bookshop in Kista.

He felt fake and stupid as he gave it to Elsa, but she was touched, and that was what mattered.

40

The history of the world ended, and continued. At school, where the staff had once worried what would happen when the proportion of those who had moved there from other countries exceeded thirty percent, the children with roots in the People's Home now constituted two percent of pupil numbers. But the staff body was intact, and Ragnar was still there in his wood workshop.

Swedish Telecom was privatized; the gray telephones were replaced by a range of other colors and designs; TV channels grew in number and became more vividly colored; the schools competed for pupils and the post office for letters.

Ragnar Johansson, who esteemed competitive sport so highly, did not esteem this. To anyone who would listen—Elsa, however, had just moved to a bedsit with kitchenette near Brommaplan, which she had got from the Housing Agency after three years and eleven months in the queue—he said ruefully and wearily: "How idiotic is it for two different people to run up and down stairs in every block of flats when one can do it perfectly well?"

Only his wife Elisabet heard him, and she agreed with those who wrote in the newspaper that competition was good and did not care how many people went running up and down the stairs as long as the post arrived.

Ragnar lived alone with her in the house that had grown too large for them. It had slowly dawned on him that he could not live the rest of his life like this.

To have somewhere to channel his energies, he set up a club among the staff at school. The emblem of membership was the wearing of a tie every Friday. In all the years he had been working, since the early 1950s, he had never worn a tie for work, not even in the days when state employees at lower grades wore them on a daily basis, because his could easily get caught in the lathe or sanding machine. But at the first meeting of the club, he declared that there was a greater risk nowadays of his being throttled by a pupil than by his own tie. Twice in the past year his life had been threatened, first by a boy in Year 9, and then by a former pupil on behalf of a younger brother. Nothing had happened except that he had been petrified.

The club went out for a few beers from time to time. At those sessions he would smoke a sly cigarette or two, to remind himself of his pipe-smoking youth. Elisabet encouraged him to do things with his colleagues and was pleased that he seemed a bit brighter again, after those dismal years since the children had taken charge of their own futures.

He even joined an art society in Blackeberg to fill a few evenings and reconnect with his old admiration for the visual arts, especially Matisse, whose sheer simplicity had always impressed him.

The society had a program of guest speakers, and life-drawing classes and painting lessons were also included. A woman who was a fellow art enthusiast and went to all the exhibition openings to which the members received special invitations paid him a good deal of attention and seemed appreciative, too. She always took the place next to his and laughed at things he said, which no one had found amusing before. The woman was recently divorced, it transpired, although she did not seem cast down by this but cheerful and energetic, as if divorce had reinvigorated her.

Ragnar started looking forward to art society meetings and invested in some new shirts and two pairs of trousers of a more modern cut than those he usually wore.

When he had been a member for six months, the society arranged a group visit to Paris. They would visit the Louvre and the Musée Picasso with their own Swedish-speaking guide.

Ragnar had never been to Paris. He felt extremely unsure whether he ought to go, anticipating what would happen there. It was in a bid for permission to do the inevitable yet unthinkable that he asked his wife several times whether she really thought he ought to join the tour. If she gave her approval, he could almost convince himself that she had consented to being left. For if what was going to happen did happen, then he would leave Elisabet, because he could not cope with uncertainty and ambivalence, even temporarily.

The trip coincided with the Easter holidays, and Elisabet said that of course he should go. They had mainly stuck to tours of Swedish villages and sad little towns in recent decades, apart from the two driving holidays in mainland Europe.

She encouraged him to do everything that would give him pleasure.

So he went. And in Paris the thing happened that Ragnar knew he could not escape. The woman was called Ingrid, and Ragnar lost his head, put aside his discipline, austerity, and firmness and went with the flow.

For one last time in his life, he wanted to experience a little happiness, freedom, and intoxication. Everyone had let him down and now he was going to let them down, too.

But the anguish when he returned home and took his place in the marital bed was overwhelming. He could not bear himself and did all he could to ensure the blame was shared equally by his wife. If he acted like a man wronged then maybe he was one, so that was what he did. He developed a taste for the idea that you are whatever you say and feel yourself to be, and that everything is subjective and relative, as his son Erik used to say.

He secretly carried on seeing Ingrid for the months that followed. They held hands and kissed over café tables and in restaurants to which none of his acquaintances would ever go.

Ragnar had started listening to people who said that the world was ruled by feelings and that this was a good thing. Feelings were the only certainty, the only thing anybody could know about, they told him, and he repeated it to himself like something that ought to have occurred to him sooner.

When something starts to roll, it has to carry on rolling. The People's Home placed special demands on its citizens, and it could not have lasted forever, or even for very long. Decrees and prohibitions had to be more generally observed if they were to endure. Like everything else, it had its own half-life and disintegration built into it.

After three months of subterfuge, Ragnar asked for a divorce. He let go, allowed his principles to crumble and duty to be cast into the dirt.

His wife Elisabet Berg entered a period of profound shock. It was so profound as to be detectable only in the fact that her physical movements took on a mechanical look. In the very first week, she applied to remove Johansson from her person and revert to her maiden name, which she had never entirely thrown off but retained as a mental precaution and a memory of who she had been.

For some years afterwards, she lived in a small, shabby, rented flat in Johanneshov. It was a bad time to sell a house. Interest rates were high, and state finances were depleted by decades of generosity and rising expectations.

After announcing his intention to seek divorce, Ragnar went on his own to weekend flat viewings, looking for somewhere for Elisabet to live, somewhere that would be worthy of her.

But no dwelling could be worthy of her, because the only possible candidate was the one she already lived in, from which she had now been ejected.

Mother Svea was brokenhearted about her son. By the time Gunnar was the age Ragnar had reached now, he walked with a stick like the other sixty-year-olds, a stick with a silver top, which Svea would still occasionally take out and look at.

"You can't go on like that at your age," she told Ragnar, but received no reply. He did not justify himself in any way except by saying that the world was ruled by feelings, that these were his and he intended to follow them.

The problems he had always had with Elisabet could not be described in words but were totally obvious. Even if he'd had the words for them, they would have been too hurtful to express.

Her flexibility and capacity for adapting to whatever the situation demanded was said to be the future, whereas

Ragnar's monolithic self and sharp delineations were the past, a time the collected knowledge of the world now deemed obsolete. There were no cohesive units anymore, it was said, and no monolithic egos.

He wanted to rid himself of the despot who had ruled him, his own fiercely guarded uniformity, his carefully patrolled boundaries. He thought that it had perhaps been Elisabet and the children who had forced him to become the person he had been, exact and hard and bossy. Now it was time to cast off that guise and step into a new one.

Just as he had adopted forward movement even though he believed in his heart in eternally determined and perfected forms, and had mistaken modernity for such a state of being, he once again tried to adopt what was new.

It turned out to be a convulsive business, because he was singularly ill-suited to the fragmentary, divided, unclear, and dissolving approach that was now coming in, as he soon realized. Indignantly and with a kind of desperation he asked Elsa how it was possible for this internet, w-w-w-w-w as he called it, sarcastically feigning a stutter, could work when there was no one regulating it. Where was it, where in the world was it located, and whose hand was on the controls? There had to be something solid behind it.

He also asked her how people could accept that new technology meant you could tell who was calling you on the phone. He felt the old, unchanging shame burn in his body at the thought that individuals, particularly

Erik and Elsa, saw his number on the display and decided not to pick up. How could that be right and desirable, he thought, when in all other contexts it was wrong not to treat everyone the same?

Elsa could not come up with an answer for him that was both trustworthy and considerate.

A world with no center was not for Ragnar Johansson. And yet he had yearned to let go of the old order and his place in it, in the hope that human beings lacked a fixed nature and core, as was now being claimed, and could reinvent themselves exactly as they fancied.

41

R agnar and Ingrid had moved in together, in a big new flat in Vällingby, and they started painting pictures. He painted so many that there was barely room for them in his new place of residence. The man with the set square, folding rule, and compasses was to be banished, the one who gave orders and searched for the essence of things. He would blow up the craftsman's prison of reason and rules.

After two months, he stopped abruptly, because he could see he was no good. Then he packed away the easel that he had made himself, believing it to be his final piece of craftsmanship, carried it down to the basement and went back to his own material, wood. He went over to the frenzied production of sculptures, boxes of all sizes, wall clocks, trivets, and ornaments, which he then sold to the arts and crafts shops around the city, as he had for a brief period in his youth.

The difference now was that he decorated everything he made with painted flowers. All his pieces were positively strewn with flowers, and it occurred to him that perhaps his real self was to be found in that blossom and warmth, not in the cube of granite into which he had previously forced it. He convinced himself he had suppressed his floral side through an entire life of duty and self-sacrifice.

It was much defamed in those days, his hard rectangularity. It was a defamation that ill became him.

His little summer place in Roslagen, where everything had once been conceived in lasting combinations intended for eternity, now appeared to him through new eyes, and together with Ingrid he covered up the old elements as far as possible, introducing adaptations so the corners were more rounded and the functionalism less glaring; making whatever small alterations could be made to disturb the house's intentional inalterability.

He tried to absorb the idea that was on everyone's lips nowadays, even at staff development days with the new, forward-looking principal at school, that nothing had to be as it was but could just as well be some other way, if people would only drop their prejudices.

Because Ragnar had had so many clear perceptions of the natural order of things and the essential qualities of existence, there was nothing left for him but capitulation.

Thus when Elsa rang from time to time and tried to talk to him the way they used to talk, in the belief that he still thought about logical problems that were immutable in character, he never had anything to say. He had stopped thinking, stopped brooding about expressions of irrationality or the scourge of sloppiness. He just said *yes* and *you're right* and laughed uncomfortably at her attempts to discuss matters he no longer considered worth puzzling over. For where had that attitude got him? To the wasteland of disappointment. He had been wrong about everything, people told him.

In the course of their conversations the old fire was occasionally rekindled. He had noticed that the athletics commentators on TV had reverted to the old feminine forms they had abolished in his era, so women would not be consigned to their own insignificant corner. He asked Elsa—because she, after all, was engaged in linguistic research of some kind—to make them put a stop to this bad practice of referring to "medalistes" and sportswomen, female gymnasts, and lady hammer throwers.

What were they doing? Once upon a time in Sweden majoress and professoress were the titles given to the wives of a major or a professor. How could anyone respect a medaliste? You could hear a mile off that it was a lesser form of medalist.

Elsa promised to see what she could do.

Aside from this flaring of passion for what was right and true, he remained a shadow of his former self; someone who went on package holidays, jogged, drank red wine with his meals and whiskey before bed, and read the paper without thinking anything in particular about what was in it.

But whenever he went abroad, he would make a note beforehand of his destination and the names of the hotel and airline, and leave the information with Erik and Elsa. In the event of anything happening, they would not be left dangling in a state of doubt. His habit of foresight had not left him.

He always made sure to send postcards home, too, as he had done from Spain all those years ago. It seemed important to keep it up now that everything else had been scattered to the four winds.

42

A short time after the new century had dawned, Elsa invited her father to her doctoral disputation. There was a reception afterwards at the venerable Berns restaurant. Ragnar attended with some degree of misgiving.

As the disputation progressed, he found he did not understand a single whole sentence of what was being said, not one, even though they were speaking Swedish.

He had dressed in his best suit, a dark, single-breasted, well-tailored suit with a slim cut, which had not been cheap when he bought it in 1967. With it he wore a discreet silk tie, a white shirt, and some new leather shoes he had splashed out on.

There were fine speeches in his daughter's honor; everybody praised her and flocked around her, with evident understanding that enabled them to say something on the subject of Elsa's thesis. Several people came up and congratulated him, too, as her father. He did not know what he should reply, but he could hear how awkward he sounded and sense the sheepish expression on his face. Anxiety closed around his chest and he started to perspire.

He mopped his face but the sweat would not stop, pouring from his forehead and down his back.

Mop as he might, it kept on coming, and started to drip onto the floor, the beautiful wooden floor at Berns, which was laid in such elegant patterns that he devoted all his subsequent thoughts that afternoon to wondering whether he would have been able to make anything like that himself. The floor appeared to be made of oak and was well maintained; it was shiny and gleaming, although darkened by time and use.

He attempted to blink the sweat out of his eyes. His paper napkin was saturated, and he resorted to the sleeves of his jacket.

Elsa stood with a glass in her hand, talking in a relaxed and informed way to anyone who came up to her. She was keeping close to her father, and he realized that she was protecting him, trying to help. Ragnar was aware of his stiff smile, nauseated by the falseness of it, and he sweated even more.

At no point did he gain any clear insight into what the subject for which Elsa had been awarded her doctorate actually involved, though he read several times through what was written in elegant letters on thick, watermarked paper, including her name.

Finally, the sweating ended. Anxiety could no longer ride him with the same intensity, and the guests were starting to thin out. He told Elsa it was time he made a move, but stood there indecisively.

Then he told her it was clever what she had done, terribly clever. She was genius, he said. Genius was a word he used on special occasions when he wanted to give praise, a word from the old Stockholm vernacular that he and his friends in Birkastan would use when they talked to each other. *Geenyus* was how he said it.

"You're *geenyus*, Elsa," he said.

She waved a dismissive arm.

"It's not as weird as it sounds, all that stuff you heard at the disputation."

As he was about to leave, he looked out over Berzelii Park and the square at Norrmalmstorg, absently rather than with concern, and declared with the knowledge of someone bypassed by life: "I used to wax your skis. I did that."

He gave her a nod and went. Ragnar's daughter stood there, watching the hunched figure move away.

Mother Svea died in her residential care home one autumn day, two years before the end of the twentieth century, after falling and breaking her hip three months earlier. She never got up again and was confined to bed. In those last weeks she ate nothing. The whole thing had an element of nature's own business transaction: death came and introduced itself to Svea as the preferable alternative. Ever since Gunnar's death nearly thirty years before, whenever the thought came into her mind, she had been just as scared of ending up in the care home in Enskededalen as her grandmother Helena had been of ending up at Halltorp when Johannes went to America.

One day right near the end, she felt able to sit up in a wheelchair when Elsa and Elisabet came to see her. It was an afternoon visit. Rays of pale autumnal sun lit up the dust in the corners of the institution with linoleum carpets and the smell of death.

Svea drank the thin coffee from a ribbed plastic cup in small sips. Of the thousands of liters of coffee that had passed through her body in a lifetime spanning almost a century, this cup was one of the worst, but it was what she was reduced to now that she could no longer brew her own.

Coffee had been her elixir ever since the age of ten, always coffee; when she got up at four to milk the cows where she served as a farm maid, it was coffee that pulled her through. She had been in the habit of giving half a kilo of dark roast to friends and acquaintances for Christmas and birthdays, the expensive coffee from Arvid Nordquist's, which she had been so delighted to have back after the rationing of wartime.

The coffee here at the care home was so bitter and disgusting that Elsa was drinking tea. A squashed little tea bag was parked beside her cup. Svea looked at it and pulled a face.

"So you've gone all hoity-toity?"

"What do you mean?"

"Drinking tea."

Elsa looked uncomprehendingly at the plastic cup and the beverage approximating tea that was cooling inside it.

"Posh ladies drink tea," said Svea. "The rest of us drink coffee. But it isn't particularly nice, I must say."

Silence descended once more on the little company of three in the dayroom, with its sofas and armchairs of pine and unyielding foam-rubber cushions. Topics of conversation did not readily present themselves. Svea slipped in and out of lucidity. She said: "They said on TV that Göran Persson's gone up to Norrland."

"The prime minister?"

"Yes."

"But he'll be back, surely?"

"Yes, he will."

Elisabet adjusted one of the potted plants on the windowsill and noted that it needed watering. Svea observed her visitors as from a great distance, as if they belonged to a different world.

"You'll find your way to the grave, won't you? Our grave, where Gunnar and Ture are buried. You'll find it, won't you?"

"Of course we will," said Elisabet. "We've been there virtually every All Saints' Day and Easter."

"Yes," said Svea. "So we have. Ragnar's supposed to be coming in tomorrow, I think that's what he said."

The visit was over.

The day she died, they called Ragnar from the hospital to say she didn't have long. He called Elsa and they got there as fast as they could. They sat on either side of Mother Svea's bed; her eyes were closed, and Elsa clasped the gnarled, bluish hand with its thin skin.

"Farewell then, Svea. Farewell."

Mother Svea's voice was low, but the words were clearly audible.

"Farewell then, Father. I'll close the gate after you."

Ragnar and Elsa thought she had left them. They held their breath and straightened their backs. Then Svea opened her eyes, sighed and said: "Things turned out well for us in the end. They couldn't have turned out better."

Those were the final words of Svea Johansson, née Svensson.

LENA ANDERSSON is a novelist and a columnist for *Svenska Dagbladet*, one of Sweden's largest daily newspapers. Considered one of the country's sharpest contemporary analysts, she writes about politics, society, culture, religion, and other topics. Her fifth novel and English-language debut, *Willful Disregard*, was awarded the 2013 August Prize, Sweden's highest literary honor.

SARAH DEATH has translated nearly forty books, including Lena Andersson's earlier novel *Willful Disregard*. She has twice won the George Bernard Shaw Prize for translation from Swedish, and in 2014 she was inducted into the Royal Order of the Polar Star for services to Swedish literature.